KILL THE ÁMPAYA

KILL THE ÁMPAYA

The Best Latin American Baseball Fiction

EDITED AND TRANSLATED BY DICK CLUSTER

MANDEL VILAR PRESS

This book is typeset in Monotype Sabon. The paper used in this book meets the minimum requirements of ANSI/NISO Z39-48-1992 (R1997). ♾

Designed by Barbara Werden

Library of Congress Cataloging-in-Publication Data is available.

Printed in the United States of America.

16 17 18 19 20 21 22 23 / 9 8 7 6 5 4 3 2 1

Mandel Vilar Press
19 Oxford Court, Simsbury, Connecticut 06070
www.mvpress.org

For my parents, H. Raymond Cluster and
Peggy F. Cluster, who taught me to love the game.
Ray never tired of telling how, at thirteen, he saw Dolph
Luque pitch in the World Series of 1933.

CONTENTS

KILL THE ÁMPAYA

The Spanish-Speaking Baseball Countries

INTRODUCTION

I'm sitting in the Estadio Latinoamericano in Havana during the championship round of the Cuban baseball season in the spring of 1992. One of the grandstand orators so typical of Caribbean baseball crowds is holding forth, so our entire section can hear him, on topics like who ought to be selected for that year's national team, why the manager should have called for a hit-and-run, who wasn't in position to take a cutoff throw, as well as asides about daily life in that moment of Cuban history. The comment I'll never forget, though, is not one of the opinions but the punch line: «y eso lo sabe hasta un chileno que no sepa donde está la primera base»—"and anybody knows that, even a Chilean who doesn't know where to find first base."

This has stuck in my mind because it was one of my first indications of how much—not just for Cuba but for all the *países peloteros*, all the Spanish-speaking nations of the Caribbean rim that are baseball-playing countries—the sport of pitcher and catcher, diamond and outfield, fielder and base runner is perceived as an integral part of their cultures, a piece of what makes their people who they are. Whatever they share with that far-off Chilean, baseball is a part of what makes them distinct. The fact that their national sport happens to have evolved in the northern neighbor is almost an afterthought. I doubt that it was in the mind of that grandstand orator in 1992 at all. Though the word *béisbol* was imported along with the game, in common speech in Cuba and the Dominican Republic and Puerto Rico the game is always *la pelota*, which is simply the Spanish word for ball.

Yet the game's origin matters, too. Baseball has a place in the complicated love-hate relationship, power dynamics, understandings, and misunderstandings between those south of our border and ourselves, and that's another piece of what set me off on the mission of collecting and translating the stories that follow. Paradoxically, the favorite major-league team of many fans and writers, regardless of how many times they may have felt or chanted *Yanqui go home,* is often the one based in the Bronx. In these stories you'll find Yankee Stadium itself, Casey Stengel's ghost on a stifling Nicaraguan night, and cameo appearances by other pinstripe legends, too. You'll also find bets on a game between the Cardinals and the Braves placed in a Santo Domingo bar, and signings of Venezuelan would-be major leaguers by the White Sox and the Astros. You'll find some of the many and creative ways in which Caribbean-rim Spanish has adopted and adapted the English vocabulary of the game, my favorites being *aut* and *ao* for what happens when a runner is tagged with the ball, *ponchado* for the state of the batter after three whiffs, *roletazo* for a ground ball, and *cuadrangular* (as well as *homrón* or *jonrón*) for a four-bagger. And not surprisingly, US military interventions figure in two stories—once as part of a many-layered baseball origin myth and once in ironic counterpoint to the hero's love of the game.

Still, most of the stories are primarily domestic or universal. Baseball appears in the foreground or the background, as part of the local social fabric or as a metaphor for anything from existential choice to sexual orientation to divine will. Teams from rival towns compete in the bushest of bush leagues. Fans and schemers deploy supernatural powers—or are they scientific?—to swing the outcomes of professional games. A girl who wants to play in little league confronts both sexism and rural poverty. A coastal region faces floods and its ball club's fall from pennant winner to cellar dweller; is this an analogy for national politics, or is it the biblical curse of Job? After a poet and a catcher meet and dance at a party, will diamond tales or recited verses provide the sauce for their one-night stand? In the story set in Yankee Stadium, what takes center stage is the plight of an African ballplayer and the trauma in his past.

Baseball lore and literature in North America are similarly replete with ghosts, curses, rivalries, origin myths (Abner Doubleday of Cooperstown did not invent the game), and superstitions, though rarely with politics or international affairs. Still, I think Latin American eyes may see from different angles and focus on different things. But that's for you to decide. Like any pregame show host, I want to make use of the rest of this introduction to offer some history from past "seasons." Then I'll say a few more things about baseball literature and about selecting and translating these stories.

• • •

The first baseball games in the Spanish-speaking world took place in Cuba in the mid-1860s, two decades after the game had evolved out of British and American predecessors such as rounders and one-o'-cat in the environs of New York City—and at approximately the same time as Union soldiers from that metropolis were popularizing "the New York game" throughout the United States during the Civil War.

The sport came to Cuba primarily with middle- and upper-class Cubans returning from study at Catholic colleges in the United States, and perhaps also via the crews of US merchant and naval ships. Its rapid spread throughout the island was due in part to the fact that the new sport arrived just as long-simmering sentiments against both Spanish colonialism and slavery were erupting into open rebellion, sparking the Ten Years' War (1868–78), which pitted an uneasy coalition of Cuban planters, other white Cubans of all classes, free people of color, and escaped slaves against the Spanish imperial army. Both then and in the decades to follow, Cubans latched onto baseball as a modern, democratic, healthy, sportsmanlike, and distinctly non-Spanish entertainment, one that baseball's boosters explicitly contrasted to the bullfight, which they condemned as old-world, old-fashioned, bloodthirsty, hierarchical, and unfair.

The sport soon spread throughout the island among people of all classes and origins. Professional teams were founded in the cities of Havana and Matanzas, and makeshift teams and clubs flourished from docks to sugar mills, while publications such as *El Pitcher* and *El Base-ball* covered and promoted the game. Spanish authorities tried on a few occasions to ban baseball completely, but in vain. By the 1890s a visiting Spanish poet reported that "everyone was at baseball—men and women, old and young, masters and servants. . . . I had a presentiment that Spain had died for Cuba."[1]

When the final Cuban war for independence broke out (1895–98), Spanish authorities again instituted a ban, and this time professional ballplayers were among those who flocked to join the rebellion. Three members of the pitching staff of the Almendares Azules (Blues, later known as the Alacranes, Scorpions) became rebel army officers, as did players from the other clubs. Emilio Sabourín, player-manager of the rival Havana club and one of the organizers of the first professional league, was arrested for his proindependence activities and exiled to a prison camp in Spanish Morocco, where he died.

Thus, by the time US troops intervened in the Cuban-Spanish conflict in 1898, baseball was already firmly established in Cuba as a nationalist pastime, however North American its pedigree. The US troops landed as part of what was, from the northern perspective, the Spanish-American War, which resulted in Spain's cession of what was left of its historic empire—Cuba, Puerto Rico, the Philippines, and Guam—to the United States. When the *yanqui* troops ended their occupation of Cuba in 1902, the Platt Amendment (inserting a perpetual US right of intervention into the new Cuban constitution) was seen as an imposition they left behind. *La pelota* was not.

The Cuban struggle for independence also proved to be the main source of the sport's introduction to neighboring countries and peoples. From the 1860s to the 1890s, tens of thousands of Cubans left the island to escape Spanish political repression or the economic devastation resulting from the independence wars. Some settled in Tampa or New York, and others in Puerto Rico, the Dominican Republic, and the Atlantic coasts of Mexico and Venezuela. As veteran Venezuelan sportswriter Juan Vené has put it, Cuba was "the cradle of those who played the major role in introducing baseball to the rest of our countries . . . that [Cuban] blend of indigenous Tainos with Spaniards and African blacks, living ninety miles of Caribbean waters off the coast of Florida, those cheerful and talkative Caribbeans, extroverted and emigrant as people who are born and grow up on islands tend to be."[2] Sugar planters or sugar mill mechanics, doctors or dockworkers, students of professions or professional shortstops, they brought baseball knowledge, equipment, and especially enthusiasm to the cane fields surrounding San Pedro de Macorís and the streets of Santo Domingo in the Dominican Republic, to the Yucatán peninsula and the port of Veracruz in Mexico, and to Venezuela and Puerto Rico as well.

The earliest record of baseball in the Dominican Republic is a newspaper article from 1896 that records a game between two teams of Cuban sailors in the port of San Pedro de Macorís on the southern coast, where émigré Cuban investors and technical personnel had recently developed a modern sugar industry. When the *María Herrera* docked there, the sailor-ballplayers formed two teams, each under the sponsorship of a Cuban mill owner, and they played before an enthusiastic crowd of male and female Cuban residents, according to the report. Soon every mill had a team, made up primarily of Cuban and North American employees, but with increasing numbers of Dominicans as time went on. The sugar trade between San Pedro and US ports also ensured a steady supply of equipment and a way to stay abreast of the latest rules. San Pedro de Macorís has been a baseball stronghold from that day to this, producing such major-league talents as Sammy Sosa, Robinson Canó, and Alfonso and Rafael Soriano. In the Dominican capital, forty miles to the west, the first known organized teams appeared in the 1890s, again under Cuban sponsorship, in this case two blacksmith brothers who operated a forge and created a ball field alongside. These teams are said to have played their first game with a used ball acquired from US sailors at a local dock. Santo Domingo high society soon adopted the game as well, forming a number of social club teams.

In Mexico, the origins of baseball are the subject of competing regional claims, all dating to the period 1870–90, involving Cubans on the Caribbean or Gulf Coast and Americans inland or on the Pacific side. Cuban émigrés are credited with bringing the game to the port of Veracruz in 1886 and to Mérida in the Yucatán peninsula in 1890. In the case of Mérida, local tradition and some documentation accord this honor to the Urzaiz brothers, three sons of a Cuban doctor who had packed a bat and an old Spaulding baseball among their belongings when they left their homeland. They soon taught the game to other teenagers in their new town. Pickup games spread throughout the city, often played with homemade bats and with balls stuffed with henequen, the hemp-based fiber at the heart of the peninsula's export boom. Formal teams followed soon after.

In inland Mexico, however, in the town of Cadereyta Jiménez in the state of Nuevo León, a memorial arch pays tribute to the "first baseball game in Mexico," which local oral tradition says was played on July 4, 1889, by railway workers camped there while building the railroad from the city of Monterrey to Tampico on the Gulf. In this version it was the railroad's director, a Kentucky lawyer and former colonel named Joseph A. Robertson, who had packed a bat and ball and paused the advance of the rails to teach his track-laying crew and some local residents the rules of the game so as to celebrate the Fourth of July. (Robertson later became a prominent Monterrey businessman, landowner, and newspaper publisher, and one of his partners in the railroad enterprise, the ex-general and former secretary of war Jerónimo Treviño, was born in Cadereyta; whether these facts contributed to the legend is unknown.) Still other versions hold that the sport was introduced on Mexico's Pacific coast in the 1870s or '80s by the crew of a US naval vessel in Guaymas or by railroad employees on a field next to their roundhouse in Mazatlán. As for Mexico City, the first documented game there took place in 1899, pitting a team made up of Mexicans against another of residents from the North. "Los Señores" defeated "Los Místers" 51 to 49.

Cubans brought the sport into Venezuela and Puerto Rico. The first teams in the former were organized in 1895 by Emilio Cramer, a proindependence émigré Cuban tobacco manufacturer. His cigarette factory was called La Cubana, and he was soon using ball games to raise funds for the struggle at home. The first genuine star was the shortstop Emérito Argudín, a Havana college player who arrived in 1898 and excelled as a fielder, base stealer, and batsman. His accomplishments included translating the latest official rules into Spanish, founding a weekly newspaper devoted to the sport, and, in 1902, hitting four home runs in the first series between a Venezuelan team and one from outside the country, when the

Caracas team played crew members of a US gunboat, the USS *Marietta*. (The naval vessel was cruising the Caribbean after participating in the blockade of Havana during the war with Spain and then in the battle to put down proindependence rebels in the Philippines.) The sailors won the first game 16–3, and Caracas won the second 27–17, thanks in part to an Argudín grand slam. The game was played near the ship's anchorage in the port of La Guaira, in an improvised stadium where, according to Venezuela's leading baseball historian, Javier González, "vendors sold fish patties and sugar water with lemon, and great quantities of beer were drunk in the makeshift stands." The victory in the second game, especially, "unleashed an unprecedented enthusiasm for baseball in the state of Vargas," the long history of which will be told in one of the three Venezuelan stories in this volume, "The Last Voyage of Arcaya the Shark."[3]

In the case of Puerto Rico, as Juan Vené puts it, "Baseball 'invaded' two years before the North Americans, who arrived in 1898." In one version of the story, the individuals who brought the game from Cuba were the sons and nephews of a Spanish army officer previously stationed on that island. If true, this would offer further proof of a popular Cuban adage of the nineteenth century that held that "a Spaniard can get anything he wants in Cuba—except Spanish children." In any case, the first three teams were called Habana and Almendares (after established ball clubs in Cuba) and Borinquén (the indigenous name for Puerto Rico); their composition reflected their names.

Only in Panama and Nicaragua did baseball have purely North American roots. The sport probably came to Panama (then still part of Colombia) with Americans crossing the isthmus during the 1849 California Gold Rush or in the following decade with US railroad builders, travelers, and crews. The first documented game, in 1882, pitted Club Panamá against sailors from ships in port. Nicaragua, probably the last Spanish-speaking country to take up the sport, seems to have acquired it, fittingly, from the cradle of the "New York game." In Bluefields on the Caribbean coast, a lumber exporter named Albert Adlesberg sent back to his home town of New York City for baseball equipment, and by 1889 he had launched several teams. Since this part of Nicaragua was still under British domination at the time, he needed only to convert the local cricket players to the diamond game. Three years later, baseball reached the capital, Managua, as one of a number of activities sponsored by a social club for the well-to-do. The team's star pitcher had recently returned from studying medicine at New York's Fordham University, where one of the earliest Cuban players, Esteban "Steve" Bellán, had attended and starred three decades before.

• • •

Once firmly established in these three islands and three mainland countries, baseball flourished in the twentieth century as more teams formed to represent cities, towns, workplaces, social clubs, and barrios. There was amateur ball, professional ball, and ball that was somewhere in between, with gate receipts subsidizing players and equipment. Sponsors and promoters, including both industrialists and politicians, also made payments under the table, and there was also a rise of gambling on baseball, which plays a role in a number of the stories in this collection. The saga of the emergence, eclipse, and rebirth of the many professional and semipro teams and leagues in each of the countries is too complex and eclectic to try to cover here, but what is perhaps most noteworthy is how the game was local, Caribbean-wide, and linked to the United States, all at once.

Domestically, the twentieth century saw the emergence of professional and semipro rivalries as intense as any sports feuds anywhere. In Santo Domingo this meant the crosstown rivalry between tigers and lions, Los Tigres del Licey and Los Leones del Escogido; in greater Havana, between Los Alacranes of Almendares and Los Leones (again) of Habana. Nationally, especially in later periods, it was Licey vs. Los Aguilas (Eagles) of Santiago de los Caballeros in the Dominican Republic; Caracas vs. Los Navegantes de Magallanes in Venezuela;[4] Havana's Industriales vs. almost any other province in Cuba—shades of the Yankees' role in the American League—or, in Nicaragua, Managua's similarly regarded Bóer team vs. Chinandega or León. (In the earliest days of Nicaraguan ball, it was fashionable to name teams after warring nations or armies; Bóer is the only such name that survives.)

Yet at the same time, among ballplayers trying to make a living from the game, there developed a kind of international market in which players with established reputations moved from league to league and country to country according to where economic and political conditions offered the best salaries and where varying summer/winter seasons allowed. Thus, in the course of his twenty-five-year career (1922–47), Martin Dihigo—known as El Maestro and El Inmortal, and in many eyes the greatest player of all time—pitched, played every other position, too, and player-managed in his native Cuba, Mexico, Venezuela, the Dominican Republic, and Puerto Rico. He then retired to Cuba, where he became the first minister of sports under the Castro regime. Similarly, the great Dominican infielder-outfielder Juan Esteban "Tetelo" Vargas played at various times for Licey, Escogido, and San Pedro de Macorís in his native land and for teams in Venezuela, Mexico, and Puerto Rico, where he settled after retirement.

In a few cases—most famously the Cuban hurler Adolfo "Dolph" Luque, who won the last game of the 1933 World Series for the Giants after a long National League career—these international moves included the US major leagues. But most of the star players were too dark or Latin-featured to get past the major-league color bar (even the white-skinned

Luque was constantly taunted by opposing benches for his ethnicity), so they played in the US Negro leagues instead. Dihigo played for Negro league teams, including the New York Cubans and Homestead Grays. He is the only player to be enshrined in the baseball halls of fame of Cuba, Mexico, and the United States. Tetelo Vargas played for the New York Cubans, as did many other Latino players between 1935 and 1950. The team included not only Cubans but Mexicans, Puerto Ricans, and Dominicans as well. It was owned by Alejandro "Alex" Pompez, born in Key West to yet another pro-independence Cuban exile, who in this case left his entire estate to the independence organization when he died in 1896. Pompez (1890–1974) got his start in New York as a Harlem numbers banker, later served as an important New York Giants scout, and was inducted into the Hall of Fame in 2006.

The color bar, however, did not mean that there was no other contact between Latin Americans and major-league ball. In the years before free agency and television rights made baseball a high-paying profession, major-league teams played frequent exhibition games against Negro league clubs and touring Latin American teams. US teams and all-star squads likewise traveled throughout the Caribbean basin to play exhibition games, while individual players from the American, National, and Negro leagues supplemented their salaries by signing with Latin American teams for the winter season. This meant that, until the color bar came down, Latin American leagues provided US players, both black and white, with their only true experience of integrated baseball, from the dugouts to the hotels. (There were, of course, some limits, particularly in Puerto Rico and pre-1959 Cuba, where whites-only private clubs and beaches were the norm.) It meant, too, that Latin American fans had direct experience with the US leagues. While cheering wildly for their own teams when they confronted those from the North, fans also developed loyalties to major-league players or franchises, which they often followed via radio or newspapers as passionately as they followed their own.

Another aspect peculiar to the Latin American game was the episodic presence of politics. Always, of course, the victory of regular or all-star teams in international tournaments was an occasion for intense national pride, as will be reflected in a number of stories, including "How Tomboy María Learned She Could Fly" and "Apparition in the Brick Factory." Puerto Rico and the Dominican Republic vied fiercely for many Caribbean-wide titles. During the tiebreaking final game of the 1941 Baseball World Cup between traditional winner Cuba and underdog Venezuela, all schools and most shops in Venezuela were closed, the national government cabinet meeting was postponed, and the entire country listened to the radio broadcast from Havana. The victorious Venezuelan team, first to win an international championship, was ever after enshrined as the Heroes of '41 and was received with a valedictory address and poem by the popular writer and politician Andrés Eloy Blanco, represented in this volume by his classic tale of rural rivalry, "The Glory of Mamporal."

But particular teams or leagues were often sponsored for internal political purposes as well. Two very different examples will give an idea.

The first is from Yucatán, where baseball became tied to a local variant of the Mexican Revolution. As mentioned above, Yucatán had flourished as the scene of a late-nineteenth- and early-twentieth-century export boom in henequen fibers, which were made into twine that was used in the new mechanical harvesters employed in agriculture in the United States and beyond. Because of both geography and commerce, the peninsula was relatively isolated from the rest of Mexico but well linked by ship with the United States and Cuba. So the revolution came late to Yucatán, five years after the rest of the country, first under the leadership of left-leaning General Salvador Alvarado (1915–18) and then that of the elected socialist governor Felipe Carrillo Puerto (1922–24). Both attempted to break the longstanding power of a small aristocracy of landowners and exporters over the Mayan-descended farmworkers (essentially serfs) and the wealth of the henequen economy. The elite had sponsored some urban teams and paid to import Cuban players to bolster their performance, but in the small towns and plantations the laborers were forbidden to travel without permission and required to work from dawn to dusk. When a 1916 decree ended debt peonage, forced labor, and travel restrictions for some eighty thousand rural laborers, grassroots baseball was a big beneficiary, with town teams traveling to play each other and those in the cities, and every hamlet wanting its own squad. In the early 1920s, alongside the distribution of hacienda land to laborers, support of baseball was raised to the level of ideology, seen both as a way of promoting Mayan culture and as a symbol of freedom. The sport was linked to ancient Mayan games played in the ball courts being unearthed in the ruins of Chichén Itzá and other sites, and again (as in Cuba in the previous century) it was contrasted with the bullfight, a symbol of the Spanish Conquest and the prerevolution era. Further, as Felipe Carrillo Puerto put it, "Every man has a right to recreation. It will be good for their bodies, but it will be even better for their souls. . . . They have been slaves so long that they have forgotten how to play—slaves do not play; and people who play are not slaves."[5] Widespread physical education was added to school curricula, and the Socialist Party's base organization created a special sports section headed by a teacher of baseball, provided team travel subsidies to further break down the isolation of the countryside, distributed over twenty thousand US dollars' worth of baseball equipment, and organized ball clubs in more than seventy percent of the state's communities. Team names included Emiliano Zapata and (in Spanish) Agrarian Reformer, the Martyrs of Chicago, and Red Yucatán.

Carrillo Puerto was deposed and executed by the local military and the central government in 1924, but Yucatán has remained one of Mexico's fervent baseball regions. Today the Leones de Yucatán play in a Mérida stadium named after the Mayan feathered serpent deity Kukulcán—although a 2015 sale of naming rights to the US car rental company has now rendered it, officially, the "Kukulcán Alamo." Meanwhile, in 2006, as soccer eclipsed baseball in the Mexican capital, the long-time Tigres of Mexico City moved to Cancún.

At the other end of the political spectrum have been the teams promoted and subsidized by the right-wing military rulers Rafael Trujillo in the Dominican Republic, Anastasio Somoza in Nicaragua, and Juan Vicente Gómez in Venezuela (or, more specifically, his son, Colonel Gonzálo Gómez) to bolster their prestige. The most famous case is that of Trujillo, though he was not himself a baseball fan. After renaming Santo Domingo as Ciudad Trujillo in 1936, he was determined that for reasons of personal and political prestige the city should not lose another national championship to either Santiago de los Caballeros or San Pedro de Macorís. Therefore, he decreed that for the 1937 season historic capital rivals Licey and Escogido should be combined into a single team, Los Dragones (Dragons). Since his brother José was already a major investor in Licey, Trujillo put that team's general manager in charge of the new club, with unlimited cash at his disposal to outbid the rival cities not only for Cuban talent but also for stars from the US Negro leagues, to whom he would offer much higher salaries and promises of better conditions than they had known in the States.

The result was an all-star Dragones team managed by a Cuban and made up of Americans, Cubans, one Puerto Rican (Pedro "Petrucho" Cepeda, father of future San Francisco Giants great Orlando Cepeda), and a sole Dominican. Puerto Rican sportswriter Jaime Cordova has written that, though unknown to most modern fans, this was one of the best teams assembled anywhere at any time.[6] The players were frequently monitored by armed guards, and once before a crucial game they were jailed overnight to keep them away from the bars and other temptations. Ciudad Trujillo narrowly won the championship, the dictator won the bragging rights, the relieved foreign players left the next day, all the club managements found themselves drained of cash, and Trujillo decided the whole thing wasn't worth another effort. Professional ball in the Dominican Republic collapsed for the next ten years, prompting Dominican players to seek their fortunes abroad. During the next decade the torch of domestic Dominican baseball would be carried most strongly—once again—by the sugar mill–based teams of San Pedro de Macorís.

* * *

From the 1940s to the 1960s, three events changed the picture, though not the essence, of Latin American baseball: the attempt of a Mexican millionaire to start a league that would rival the American and the National, the end of systemic racial discrimination in the US majors with Jackie Robinson's debut on the Brooklyn Dodgers in 1947, and the aftereffects of the Cuban Revolution of 1959.

That the challenge to the dominance of the US major leagues should come from Mexico was logical on the one hand because of the country's size, but surprising on the other because it was the lone baseball-playing Latin country where the sport was not the dominant national pastime. Soccer was equally popular, bullfighting remained the largest spectator sport, and the strongest baseball loyalties were—following the origins discussed above—concentrated in the Pacific Coast and in the Southeast (Yucatán and Veracruz).

Nonetheless, the flamboyant millionaire Jorge Pasquel, owner of the Veracruz Azules (Blues) and a financial power in all of Mexican baseball, decided in the 1940s to reorganize

Mexico's summer league to recruit players of all colors from the Caribbean and the United States and thus to play ball of a caliber and profitability like that of the American and National Leagues. Pasquel's motives are still a subject of much dispute. Some point to national pride (and they note that, as a seven-year-old, Pasquel witnessed the bombardment of Veracruz by US warships in 1914) or integrationist motives, others to his outsized personality, and still others to his desire to boost the profile of his longtime friend and ally, Veracruz governor and then Mexican president (1946–52) Miguel Alemán. Some assert that by threatening to raid major-league rosters, Pasquel hoped to get US baseball authorities to add a Mexican team to one of the leagues and make the World Series international at last.

Whatever the case, in 1945 and '46, as players of all ethnicities returned from World War II, Pasquel sought to recruit them to play in the Mexican League. His representatives offered large signing bonuses (then mostly unknown in the United States) and generous salaries to Negro league stars who had previously played in Mexico and also to such American and National League luminaries as Ted Williams and Stan Musial (to whom Pasquel allegedly offered a fifty-thousand-dollar contract, as opposed to the thirteen thousand dollars Musial would get for 1946 from the St. Louis Cardinals). Major-league baseball responded with a ruling that any player who went to Mexico would be banned from organized baseball for five years. The baseball commissioner, Pasquel claimed, even used his influence with the United States–based equipment manufacturers to get them to refuse to fill the Mexican League's wholesale orders for bats and balls, so they had to buy their equipment piecemeal from sporting goods stores.

In the end, the Mexican League managed to recruit a few major-league stars (most notably the Giants' pitcher Sal Maglie), but not many. Further, it had become evident that the major-league color bar was about to be broken; Jackie

Robinson's signing by the Dodgers was publicly announced in the fall of 1945, and negotiations with Robinson and other players were under way before that, so this was not the moment for younger African American players to risk their future careers. Pasquel attempted to recruit Negro league catcher Roy Campanella and outfielder Monte Irvin for the '46 season, since both of them had played in his league earlier, but they had already been signed or approached by their future major-league clubs. Gate receipts failed to reach expected levels, and by 1947 the league was down from eight teams to four and the salaries of Cuban and US players were cut. The league folded in 1948, further contributing to baseball's decline in Mexico as a national sport.

Robinson's successful debut with the Dodgers in 1947, meanwhile, opened a new chapter in Latin American baseball, because major-league clubs were now willing to sign Latino ballplayers of any complexion or features. Mexico's Roberto "Beto" Ávila (known as Bobby Avila, stress on the second syllable, in the States) won the American League batting title in 1954. Cubans Orestes Miñoso (Minnie Minoso to Chicago White Sox fans) and Camilo Pascual, Puerto Ricans Victor Pellot (Vic Power) and Roberto Clemente, and the Venezuelan shortstops Luis Aparicio and Alfonso "Chico" Carrasquel all became stars in the fifties, followed by many more in the decades to come. So baseball became entwined with another aspect of Latin American–US relations: emigration and the pursuit of the American Dream, which will figure in a number of the stories in this book. Most of the successful ballplayers, though, retained their ties to their home countries, and they often continued to play or manage there in winter ball. In the 1970s Ávila was elected mayor of Veracruz, after which he became commissioner of one of the various successor Mexican leagues; the ballparks in both Veracruz and Cancún bear his name today.

Though a few Dominican players debuted in the US majors

in the 1950s, what really turned US clubs' attention to the Dominican Republic was the break in commercial and diplomatic relations with Cuba. In the sequence of Cuban economic reforms, US economic sanctions, Cuban nationalizations, and US reprisals over the period 1959–62, baseball was not exempt. In 1954 the Havana Sugar Kings had become the first Latin American franchise in a top-ranked US minor league, the Triple-A–level International League that also included the Montreal Royals (where Jackie Robinson had played in his trial year of 1946) and the Toronto Maple Leafs. In 1959, with Fidel Castro in the audience, the pennant-winning Sugar Kings beat the Minneapolis Millers of the American Association in the annual Little World Series of the top minor leagues. Castro also threw out the first ball to open the 1960 season, but the league, under pressure from Secretary of State Christian Herter, pulled the franchise and reassigned it to Newark, New Jersey. The US economic embargo soon made it impossible for players residing in Cuba to be paid in the United States, while the Cuban government eliminated professional baseball and replaced it with a state-run and officially amateur league. Cuba restricted emigration, and the departure of ballplayers for the United States was officially viewed as political defection; by the same token, under US law the only way for Cuban players to gain admittance to the States was to declare themselves political refugees. By and large, Cuban players did not do so until the 1990s, when the combination of economic depression in Cuba and the lure of astronomical major-league salaries in the United States changed the situation again. Only in 2016 did Cuba and the United States begin talks that may result in an agreement to allow Cuban players to play under circumstances somewhat like those of other Latin Americans.

In any case, the end of the Cuban pipeline brought the opening of the Dominican one, in which the trickle that began with the debuts of Oswaldo "Ozzie" Virgil and the Alou brothers, Mateo and Felipe, in 1956–60 became a flood of talent that in many ways now dominates the US game and the Dominican imagination. Pitchers Juan Marichal and Pedro Martínez are in the Hall of Fame, and Dominican-born players in the major leagues far outnumber those from anywhere else outside the United States.

Panama, meanwhile, has contributed two outstanding players (Rod Carew and Mariano Rivera), and Nicaragua, one (Dennis Martínez).

* * *

I think the foregoing history of the game's first century in the countries rimming the Caribbean is enough to provide sufficient perspective on its place in their cultures.[7] There is more to say about more recent trends affecting Latin American baseball, particularly the creation of Caribbean-based baseball academies by the big league clubs, but this history will be known to most readers, and these and other contemporary trends will be reflected in the stories themselves. Anyway, pregame shows should only go on so long. In sum, baseball is still the national pastime in the countries represented here, with the exception of Mexico, where soccer—*fútbol*—reigns supreme. Fans still follow the local teams with as much attention as they follow their own countrymen and other players in the North. So let me now just say a few words about baseball's place in Latin American literature and a few more about my selection criteria and translations. Then you can sing the national anthem of your choice and move on to playing ball.

In North America, aside from the classic 1888 poem "Casey at the Bat," baseball has taken literary form mostly in novels. In fact, baseball novels often become an author's best-known work, or the one to be made into a film, as in the cases of Bernard Malamud's *The Natural*, Mark Harris's *Bang the Drum Slowly*, Douglass Wallop's *The Year the Yankees Lost the Pennant* (*Damn Yankees* in the stage and screen versions), or W. P. Kinsella's *Shoeless Joe* (*Field of Dreams* in the film version). There have also been specialists in baseball short stories, most notably the sportswriter Ring Lardner in the 1910s and '20s.

In Latin America, by contrast, there are practically no baseball novels, despite the number of prominent novelists who have been great baseball fans—examples being Mexico's Juan Rulfo, Cuba's Leonardo Padura and Arturo Arango, Nicaragua's Sergio Ramírez, and Puerto Rico's Edgardo Rodríguez Juliá.[8] Likewise, none of the region's famous sportswriters have turned their hands to baseball stories more than once or twice.

One reason for this gap, I suspect, is that for a long time Latin American high culture looked toward Europe, while its popular culture, at least in the Caribbean and Central America, looked toward the United States. So writing about baseball was no way to make one's literary mark as a "serious" writer. Similarly, in matters of global or continent-wide trends in Spanish-language literature, the publishing powerhouses and tastemakers tended to reside in Madrid, Barcelona, or Buenos Aires, not in the baseball powerhouses of Havana, Santo Domingo, San Juan, or Caracas. Perhaps for these reasons soccer and boxing have been better represented in literature. The closest thing to a baseball novel that I know of, the Venezuelan writer and diplomat Guillermo Meneses's 1939 *Campeones*, involves both baseball and boxing, with both sports providing a window into race, class, and national identity.

Also, to the extent that US baseball fiction could have influenced Latin American writing, the dominance of Spanish publishing again raised an obstacle. According to the late Mexican dramatist Vicente Leñero, whose one-act play *Aut at Third* concludes this collection, Juan Rulfo advised him that, for baseball fiction, he should read Lardner and other US authors, since in Mexico there was not much to be found. But the translations Leñero encountered, done in Spain by translators as remote from the game as the emblematic Chilean who didn't know where to find first base, were laughable at best.[9]

Whatever the reason, what has saved Latin American baseball fiction is that prose writers and poets too have allowed their passion for the game to be expressed in the occasional story or dramatic work.[10] Padura, Arango, and Ramírez, in addition to Leñero, are all represented here, as are the poets Camila Hernández Peña from Cuba and Alexis Gómez Rosa from the Dominican Republic. So are younger generations of writers, both female and male, such as Sandra Tavárez and Daniel Reyes Guzmán in the Dominican Republic, Yolanda Arroyo Pizarro and Cezanne Cardona in Puerto Rico, and Rodrigo Blanco Calderón and Salvador Fleján in Venezuela.

Generally, this process of venturing into baseball as a subject matter has been spontaneous, with the stories appearing in volumes of the authors' short fiction or sometimes in magazines. In the Dominican Republic, it has also, thankfully, had official support. In 2008, observing that although "baseball has been an inseparable part of Dominican national identity" there had been an "almost inexplicable absence of a body of writing that would make use of literary situations that emerge from this sport,"[11] the Secretariat of Culture of the Dominican Republic sponsored a prize contest for such stories, the winners of which were published in a collection called *Jonrón 600* in honor of the exceeding of that milestone by Sammy Sosa's career total (609). The experiment was repeated the following year, producing a new collection entitled *Círculo de espera* (On-deck circle). In 2005 and 2007 the Mexican division of the Spanish publisher Alfaguara and the Cuban publishing house Editorial Unicornio bucked the longstanding trend by publishing anthologies of their countries' baseball writing, *Pisa y corre* (Tagging up, primarily poetry, memoir, essay, and drama) and *Escribas en el estadio* (Scribes in the stadium), respectively.

For this anthology I chose a selection of the best works in a literary sense—a subjective judgment, of course—and one that is balanced in terms of nations of origin. There are five pieces each from Cuba and the Dominican Republic, three from Venezuela, three from Puerto Rico, and one each from Mexico and Nicaragua. (If there is baseball fiction from Panama, I was not able to find it.) I also sought to balance the predominant themes that appeared among the sixty-odd stories I had collected. Chronologically, all the works are from 1989 (Padura's "The Wall") or later, with the exception of "The Glory of Mamporal" (1935, but such a classic and with such staying power in Venezuela that it was made into a movie sixty-two years later, in 1997). I rejected some excellent stories because they were too densely packed with local allusions that would be Greek to US readers (that would "leave you in China," as the Cuban figure of speech says). In all the translations I've tried to provide some inconspicuous help with local references by introducing a few glosses that I hope will not interrupt the flow of the story. In the case of the Dominican Republic, it's often said that the country's twin passions are baseball and politics. So, in a brief introduction to "The Real Thing" I offer a guide to the main allusions to political history; about "The Strange Game of the Men in Blue," let me just say that in my view it's a sort of foundation myth, not a literal history, and all the more interesting for being so.

A challenging and enjoyable part of the translation process has been capturing some of the flavor of Latin American baseball terminology. In the original Spanish the writers adopt a wide variety of ways of spelling English-derived baseball terms—sometimes using English spelling (italicized or not), or sometimes using Spanish spellings that best approximate the way the word is locally pronounced. Thus *dogoa* is the best approximation of dugout, because the spelling *dug-*

out in Spanish would be pronounced as "due-goat," except that final *t*s are extremely rare. *Quetcher* and *flai* render the English sounds quite well, while *jit* does not do so exactly (the *j* sounds something like a German or Hebrew *ch*), but it's better than the silent *h* that would leave hit to be pronounced as "it." On the other hand, a writer's use of *hit* or *catcher* communicates something else, which is a character or narrator's knowledge of English or the writer's interest in reproducing it verbatim. Still another part of the flavor comes from the inventions that have renamed baseball concepts purely in Spanish. Examples include *jardinero* (a gardener, or someone standing in a yard or lawn) for outfielder; *cuadrangular* (four-angled and thus four-sided) for a hit that lets you circle the bases; *emergente* (someone who emerges, who puts in an appearance) for pinch hitter; or *imparable* (unstoppable) as an alternative to *jit*.

What I've opted to do is scatter all these sorts of usages through the stories, in italics, but much less frequently than they appear in the originals. I hope that this serves not to interrupt your reading while reminding you that the stories were not originally written in English and that Spanish baseball talk has a tropical flavor all its own. When you find a normal English word in italics, that means that the English word was used in the original. Where what's in italics is something else, then I'm preserving the Spanish spelling or the Spanish invention.

And now, *¡Pleibol!*

DICK CLUSTER
Oakland, California

NOTES

1. Louis A. Pérez Jr., *On Becoming Cuban: Identity, Nationality, and Culture* (Ecco, 1999), 83.

2. Translated from Juan Vené, *Juan Vené en la pelota* (Biblioteca Últimas Noticias, 2005), 53.

3. Javier González, *El Béisbol en Venezuela* (Fundación Bigott, 2003), 21.

4. Los Navegantes de Magallanes (Magellan's Mariners) are based in the city of Valencia, but they are always referred to as Magallanes, and I've left them that way in the story translations as well.

5. The Carrillo Puerto quote, like most of the information about baseball during the revolutionary period in the Yucatán, is drawn from Gilbert M. Joseph, "Forging the Regional Pastime: Baseball and Class in Yucatán," in *Sport and Society in Latin America: Diffusion, Dependency, and the Rise of Mass Culture*, edited by Joseph L. Arbena (Greenwood Press, 1988).

6. Jaime Córdova, *Béisbol de Corazon* (Ediciones Callejón, 2006), 99. Córdova notes that the lineup included future US Hall of Famers Josh Gibson (the "Black Babe Ruth"), James "Cool Papa" Bell (who once stole two hundred bases in a 175-game season), and Satchel Paige, as well as first baseman–manager Lázaro Sálazar (Cuba's 1934 batting champion, with an average of .407, and, during his long career, also a star in Mexico and the Negro leagues). The starting lineup included seven winners of batting championships in their respective leagues plus the pitching ace, Paige, possibly the best of all time. That Trujillo did not also attempt to recruit white players from the US majors was presumably because the championship was played during the summer season, and thus he desired to avoid a confrontation with his allies in the US government.

7. A multitude of books, articles, and websites treat Latin American baseball history in both Spanish and English. Whenever possible, I've tried to confirm information by means of a variety of sources and to compare what is written by baseball historians with that by historians of other sorts. Besides the works cited in this introduction, see "Further Reading" for some more books on the history in English.

8. Rodríguez Juliá wrote a well-known collection of Puerto Rican baseball anecdotes and minibiographies called *Peloteros*, and a climactic scene of his 2011 novel *La piscina* involves a boy attending a game in San Juan's stadium with his father, and the microcosm of class, race, and international hierarchy that he observes. Padura's wide-ranging novel *Herejes,* also from 2011, features fictional use of historical characters ranging from Rembrandt in seventeenth-century Amsterdam to the Jewish refugees on the ocean liner *St. Louis* in Havana harbor in 1939; the Cuban American outfielder Orestes "Minnie" Miñoso likewise appears. Neither would bear excerpting very well, though I asked Rodríguez Juliá just in case, and he said "nobody would understand a thing." By some strange diamond coincidence, however, 2011 also saw the publication of Puerto Rican novelist and poet Rafael Acevedo's intricate mock-Chinese novel-within-a-novel, *Flor de Ciruelo y el viento*, from which I have excerpted the unexpected baseball piece, "Clock Reaches the Emperor's Citadel."

One of the few Mexican short stories about baseball is the late Daniel Sada's "Cualquier altibajo," which, like the Venezuelan "Glory of Mamporal," is about a game in the countryside; unfortunately, I could not get permission from Sada's estate to include it. The fiction writer and essayist Carlos Velazquez, who writes in the context of the violence of the northern border states, has a recent thirty-page novella called "La jota de Bergerac" about a transvestite prostitute who is put to use as a kind of good luck charm for a visiting Cuban ballplayer.

9. See Leñero's essay "Lanzamientos para un prólogo" in *Pisa y corre: Beisbol por escrito*, edited by Vicente Leñero and Gerardo de la Torre (México: Alfaguara, 2005).

10. The poets have celebrated baseball in their own genre, too. Anthologies of baseball writing published in Venezuela and in Mexico feature poetry as prominently as prose, those from the latter country including Alberto Blanco's epic "La vida en el diamante." Nicaraguan Horacio Peña wrote a book-length poem in honor of Roberto Clemente after the Puerto Rican star's death in a plane crash while delivering earthquake relief supplies to Managua. Cuban poet Nicolás Guillén's odes on the deaths of prominent figures include one in honor of Martín Dihigo. On a lighter note, Guillén's poem "Tú no sabe inglé'" laments the troubles of a would-be gigolo hampered by his limited English, which consists only of *etrái guan* and *guan tu tri*; the verse was translated by Guillén's friend Langston Hughes as "'Merican gal comes lookin' fo' you / an' you jes' runs away / Yo' English is jes' *strike one*! / *strike one* and *one-two-three*."

11. Translated from the introduction to *Jonrón 600* by Luis R. Santos. For full bibliographic information, see "Further Reading" at the end of this book.

SWIMMING UPSTREAM

Eduardo del Llano
(Cuba)

Eduardo del Llano (born in Moscow, 1962) lives in Havana, where he founded and directed the theatrical/literary group NOS-Y-OTROS *(1982–97). His prolific literary work includes poetry, short stories, and novels in genres ranging from science fiction to detective fiction, children's literature, and literary fiction and has received prizes in both Cuba and Italy. In addition, he has written and directed several award-winning films and participated in film festivals around the globe. His latest novel, Bonsai, was published in 2014.*

"I don't like ballet," the doctor admitted.

"Okay," Nicanor said, "but it's different with me. It's not that I don't like sports, it's that they don't make any sense to me. Like I wouldn't understand a salmon explaining why it has to migrate. I just don't get a stadium full of people screaming with enthusiasm or outrage about eight guys who can bang a leather ball around better than the other eight."

"Nine."

"Whatever. The point is that a playing field doesn't leave

any room for the spirit. An artist has talent, no doubt about that. So does a mathematician. But a ballplayer just runs or hits better than an ordinary guy. Tell me what that has to do with humanity."

Nicanor was Rodríguez's patient, but Rodríguez was out on leave. To describe Nicanor, suffice it to say he was skinny and bald with bad skin. Right away, part of the doctor took a dislike to him. The other part tried to be professional.

"Sports are a lot more than that. They're struggle, strategy, teamwork. When a sprinter sets a record, when a guy jumps two and a half meters as if he were made of rubber, there's beauty in that. It's about surpassing human limits."

"Okay, but in the wrong direction. You're saying struggle and strategy. That's the language of war."

With apparent nonchalance the doctor closed his newspaper, covering the sports page to which it had been turned. He checked his watch.

"O'Donnell, you didn't come here to tell me your opinion about sports. That's not a problem in itself. Maybe the fact that your position is so rabid, so reductionist . . ."

"I came to see you, doctor, because sometimes my soul leaves my body and reappears in the body of a baseball player in a tight situation."

The doctor nodded ever so slightly, holding the patient's eyes until he blinked.

"Your soul migrates. What did you say earlier about salmon?"

"Nothing," the patient said curtly. "You're not getting rid of me by telling me my mother forced me to eat fish when I was a boy. Which, by the way, isn't true. What is true is that sometimes for a moment I transubstantiate into a baseball star."

The doctor felt a brief attack of envy. One of these days, he thought with annoyance, I'll have to ask Rodríguez to analyze me.

"What team?"

"Havana. The Industriales."

"I see. And under what circumstances does this occur? Sometimes the most ordinary things can provoke fantasies. Fatigue, for instance, or problems with your wife, or sniffing ten or twelve lines of . . ."

"The weird thing is, it doesn't happen to me. It happens to them. Typical situation: the Industriales have their backs to the wall at the end of the ninth inning, down three runs, but with the bases loaded and their last hope at bat. In that situation, it's almost a sure thing that my soul is going to take part in the game."

"And you strike out."

"No. I hit a spectacular *jonrón*. The whole time I'm conscious of being an intruder in a foreign body. I've got this tension, you know, like I'm about to be found out. The way to dissolve the tension is by swinging. Generally I hit it out of the park."

"And the player's soul? Where does it go in the meantime? Into your body?"

"For me to answer that, you'd have to prove that baseball players have souls. Anyway, the thing isn't that symmetrical. My body faints. Maybe the ballplayer's soul sits in the grandstand and watches."

"And does your soul choose to emigrate into any player in particular?"

"It used to, but he left the country. In fact, I think it's thanks to my soul that he's a major league star today. But the thing doesn't work over such a long distance, so now he's got to take care of himself."

The doctor twisted the table lamp so its beam pointed at the other man. He began waving a pencil.

"Concentrate on this. You're getting tired. Your eyelids are heavy. You want to sleep. When I say one-two-three, you'll fall into a deep sleep. One. Two. Three. What do you feel?"

"I'm a big fish. I'm swimming against a cold current."

"A salmon?"

"No, a *manjuarí*."

"The Cuban pike? But pike don't migrate."

"How should I know that? I'm just a fish, I do what my instinct tells me. If you want to discuss ichthyology . . ."

"All right, you're a pike and you're migrating. What's happening now?"

"I'm in the sea. On shore there's a group of boys playing baseball."

"The *manjuarí* lives in fresh water."

Nicanor shook his head and shrugged his shoulders.

"So hypnosis isn't going to work. Give it up."

The part of the doctor that disliked the patient now hated him intensely, and that part had become much larger. He checked his watch again.

"Look, your case isn't as unusual as you think. It's true that a Cuban who doesn't like baseball is an aberration, but on a deeper level, what are we dealing with here? Rejection and fascination, desire and taboo. It's a clear case of what we could call . . ."

"Turn on the television."

"What?"

"Obviously you don't believe me. I came here today for a reason. Everybody—even me—knows the championship series just got under way and the first game is being played right now, here in Havana, against Pinar del Río. You've already looked at your watch several times. I know you're dying to know the score, to watch. Turn on the TV."

The doctor did as he was told.

The Industriales were about to lose. It was the bottom of the ninth, and they were three runs down, but they had the bases loaded. A sinewy light-skinned black man stood in the batter's box.

"Watch," Nicanor said, and fainted.

A subtle change seemed to come over the batter. He glanced around as if disoriented. The way he was gripping the bat didn't even look right.

So what, the doctor thought. Naturally the batter is nervous. It'll take more than this, Nicanor O'Donnell, to get me to fall for the act you're putting on.

The pitcher delivered a wide, lazy curve.

Thwack.

The doctor had never seen such a stupendous blast. The ball was still gaining altitude when it cleared the scoreboard. All four players trotted home as the stands went wild. When the batter reached the plate, he leaned over, stared triumphantly at the camera, and drew something in the dirt next to the batter's box.

A fish.

That was all. Nicanor woke up.

"Now do you believe me?"

It took the doctor almost a full minute to unclench his jaw.

"That was . . . wow, I have to admit . . ."

"Impressive, right?"

"And you want these . . . episodes . . . to cease?"

"Of course not, doctor. What are you talking about? I want you to back me up scientifically. I'm planning a conversation with the Industriales management about charging them for my interventions. The fact is, whatever they've accomplished, it's thanks to me."

"But you hate sports."

"I detest them. But it would be stupid not to take advantage of this phenomenon."

A faint smile appeared on the doctor's face.

"Agreed. Come back tomorrow."

As soon as Nicanor left the room, the doctor pressed a button on his intercom.

"The patient who just left my office is dangerous. He must be committed at once. Keep him isolated, make sure he can't listen to the radio or watch television. Above all, make sure he doesn't fall asleep, even for a minute, until I say so. If he looks like he's losing consciousness, give him a good jolt of electricity."

The doctor cut off the intercom and stared into space.

He whispered, "Pinar del Río, go team, all the way."

SACRIFICE

Sandra Tavárez
(Dominican Republic)

Sandra Tavárez was born in Santiago de los Caballeros and is a graduate of that city's Universidad Tecnológica in accounting. Her story collections Matemos a Laura, Límite invisible, *and* En tiempos de vino blanco *were published in 2010, 2012, and 2016, and her work has appeared in periodicals and anthologies in the Dominican Republic and Spain. She has won honorable mention in five short story competitions, including the two national Concursos de Cuentos Sobre Béisbol (2008 and 2009).*

"If you love me, you've got to promise you'll forget this damn game forever, or else I'm calling off the wedding and accepting my father's plan to go live in Morocco, and you won't be there when the baby is born."

When you see his eyes drop, a hint of triumph shows on your face. Holding your hands, he says, "But honey, we're in the finals. We have to support the team. Why don't we go with the boys and watch today's game and then you can decide. . . ."

You look at him and think about it. The boys . . . those

two shiftless adolescents whose speech seems limited to batting averages, earned runs, RBIs, and who's on the disabled list . . . that pair who monopolize the television and, by the time they leave, have turned Arturo's apartment into a disaster zone. The same ones who call you selfish and manipulative, without considering that you're turning your back on the comfort of diplomatic life in Casablanca with your family to stay by your boyfriend's side. Still, as a sign of empathy—or, really, of sacrifice—you accede to the invitation.

It took some ball-busting on his part to get an extra ticket. His friends are surprised to see you show up in the grandstand wearing the team colors. You feign interest in learning the basic rules of the sport. Arturo goes on at length to satisfy your newfound curiosity while he tries to forget that his team is being held scoreless in what could be their last game of the season.

Suddenly all the fans are on their feet, singing and dancing for no apparent reason. In the midst of the uproar you ask why they're doing this.

"It's the *Lucky-seven*," one of Arturo's friends says.

The jargon means nothing to you.

"The seventh inning is the fortunate one," Arturo explains. "You'll see, we're going to get something going."

Indeed, the first player to stand in the batter's box sends the ball rolling toward the shortstop, who can't handle it, so the runner is now standing on base. The next batter draws a walk and slowly trots toward first. Since the teams are separated by only two runs and the next batter is the most dangerous one in the lineup, the pitching coach of the opposing team calls for time, comes to the mound, holds a small meeting with the players gathered from around the diamond. When the conversation is over, the pitcher gets ready and then throws a curve ball whose descent is interrupted by contact with the bat of the powerful hitter. Automatically your eyes follow the path of the ball. You see it bang against the fence beyond the outfield. You see the center fielder run after it, grab it, and quickly get rid of it. You watch the runners who were on first and second reach *home*, the first on his feet and the second diving in head first.

You're surprised to find yourself on your feet, screaming and dancing in time to the music blasting from the loudspeakers.

With the score tied at two runs each, the opposing team decides to replace their pitcher. You take advantage of the break to drink some water and catch your breath. The following batters are retired one, two, three, unable to score the runner from second base.

The cacophony of the crowd does not abate, and you are not immune. You let yourself float in the human wave that washes over you. You get up along with everybody else and lift your hands in the air and then let them float down, again and again.

Now, in the bottom of the ninth, the home team has runners at the corners with one out and the next batter standing in the box. There's tension in the air. You turn your cap so the brim is in the back; you clasp your hands tightly as if requesting divine intervention. The pitcher gets ready and, when he lets go of the ball, it's as if the runner on third were impelled by the same spring, taking him toward *home*. The batter makes contact. In a desperate effort, the first baseman gets to the ball and fires it toward the catcher. The umpire, crouching behind the plate, crosses his arms and then extends them to the sides.

Everybody leaps from their seats. Over the loudspeaker, for the first time, tomorrow's game is announced.

You feel Arturo's arms around you, tightening, and then lifting you in the air. Holding you up, he kisses you, and then he exults, "We won, we won, we won!"

You look at him. His eyes are gleaming in a way you've never seen, with an indefinable excitement. You could swear you've never seen him so happy before. You don't tell him yet, but you've made your decision. If he wants to marry you and watch his son grow up, he'll have to promise to forget about baseball forevermore.

APPARITION IN THE BRICK FACTORY

Sergio Ramírez
(Nicaragua)

Sergio Ramírez (Masatepe, 1942) has published the novels Castigo divino (1988, winner of the Dashiell Hammett Prize), Un baile de máscaras (1998, Prix Laure Bataillon, France), Margarita, está linda la mar (1998, Premio Alfaguara, Spain, and Premio Latinoamericano, Casa de las Américas, Cuba), La fugitiva (2011, Premio Metropolis Azul, Canada), and others. For his lifetime literary career he was awarded the Premio Iberoamericano de Letras José Donoso (Chile, 2011) and the Premio Internacional Carlos Fuentes (Mexico, 2014). His collected stories were published by the Fondo de Cultura Económica, Mexico, in 2014. He served as vice president of Nicaragua from 1984 to 1990.

The night of the apparition that changed my life keeps coming back to me now, as I sit here without a wheelchair that would at least let me move around within the confines of the church the way I would like, because the Red Cross keeps promising one to Doña Carmen, but they never come through.

Doña Carmen is getting on in years, but she's the one among my parishioners who is most attentive to me, bringing me something to eat when she can, washing me, stuck the way I am in this wooden chair, not because of any accident that left me paralyzed, nothing like that, but because my sheer obesity has made it harder and harder for me to move and now I've gotten to a point where I can't stand up, just trying to get to my feet makes my heart race like crazy in my bloated body, my ravaged face, a sick, overweight man like Babe Ruth when he got old, because he had heart trouble just like me, cleanup hitters tend to end this way, it's well known that a slugger's ability to power the ball four hundred feet over the fence into the night's darkness depends on getting the right food, which is why in my glory days I had more than enough to eat, I mean the people in charge of our national team had cases of food delivered to my house along with dietary supplements like Ovamaltina and Sustagén.

But all that's long gone now, all gone in the whirlwind, swept up like litter from the street, and what I've got left is the fat, just the fat because my muscles went slack and soft and I'm saddled with this useless reservoir that's slowly wearing me down. Once, back when I could still walk, though clumsily, I went to the Eastern Market with my string shopping bag to bargain my way through the stalls, and a butcher woman who was selling pigs' heads on the sidewalk saw me go by, stuck her nose out between the heads hanging on their hooks, grabbed hold of the haunches of a whole pig carcass and shouted happily at the top of her lungs, "That fatso would be good for more than one can of lard!" And then another one chimes in, an older woman who's got a knife in her hand, peeling yuccas under the shade of a big colored umbrella, "Don't you know that tub of lard was a great hitter in his day?" to which the one with the pigs' heads answers, "What the hell is that to me?" and the two of them double over in mirth.

The apparition came in 1956, when I was fourteen. In those days I lived for baseball, I'd bat rocks I picked up in yards and streets, or green oranges I stole from orchards that exploded right on contact, I was the proud owner of a canvas glove I'd stitched together myself, and I was never far away from the radio that belonged to Don Nicolás, the coffee grower who lived in the corner house there in Jinotepe, across from the Santiago brick factory where I worked, and it didn't matter what game was on, I'd listen. It might be Sucre Frech calling the pro games here in Nicaragua, or it might be the Gillette Cavalcade of Sports bringing us the World Series between the New York Yankees and the Brooklyn Dodgers, narrated by Buck Canel, his voice filled with that immense calm even in the most dramatic moments, that voice coming and going like a pendulum because the local stations got it from the short wave, so when the pendulum swung the other way only Don Nicolás could hear what the voice said because he'd put his ear right up against the radio in his living room and then he'd repeat everything to the crowd of shirtless boys gathered on the walk outside.

But I confess that my worst addiction was to the pictures of Big League players that came in the wrappers of peppermint and cinnamon gum. If they were Mickey Mantle or Yogi Berra they had stratospheric value in the trades we made, but there were some others nobody cared about, you could even find them thrown away in the gutter, like maybe a Carl Furillo or a Salvatore Maglie, which was unfair, I don't know why they were so despised, maybe because they played for the Dodgers and in our neighborhood around the brick factory we were all Yankees fans, but another injustice was to undervalue the pictures of Casey Stengel, even though he was the Yankees' manager, maybe that was because he looked so sour, sometimes even comical, doing nothing but sitting in the dugout watching the game, giving orders and taking notes in his little book, so no matter how many times I explained that he was a real baseball sage who had led the Yankees to straight world championships, there was no way to change anybody's opinion, pigheaded the way they were, which is all the proof you need to show that in baseball wisdom doesn't always bring admiration, that the pathway to fame is to bang the ball out of the park, steal bases, and come up with spectacular catches, you know.

But Casey Stengel, I'll never forget what the old man said to a group of reporters before the fifth game of the World Series in 1956, the year I'm talking about. He said, "I'm starting Don Larsen and I'm not changing pitchers, shit, I'm not going to dirty my shoes walking to the mound to ask him for the ball, because he's going to throw a complete game and, listen up, you assholes, Don has got balls the size of ostrich eggs and if he doesn't win this game, I'll cut off my own." And he was right. In the second game of that series, Larsen couldn't get through two innings, he got chased by the Dodgers' artillery, but then in the fifth one he came out of nowhere to throw his historic perfect game, and as soon as he got that final out, Don Nicolás, who knew baseball better than anyone, he kept his own scorebook and had all these records inside his head, he came out on the sidewalk and we could see he was really moved, and he told us, "Look at that, boys, the most imperfect of pitchers is the one who throws a perfect game."

The apparition came on a night in November, the month after that World Series which brought the Yankees yet another championship. I'd gone out to the factory yard to take a leak, the way I always did, letting my stream water the cactus fence, stark naked except for some shoes without any laces because the heat in the storeroom was stifling so I always went to bed without anything on, with no choice but to breathe the cloud of gray dust that hung in the air because this was the room where they stored the bags of Canal brand cement that went into the brick mix. So, naked like that I was pissing like I'd never stop, with the same heavy noise that horses make, when

I turned my head and that's when I saw him. Casey Stengel. Lit up by the full moon just like the light towers of Yankee Stadium.

His pinstriped flannel uniform looked impeccable, and his spiked shoes were well shined, I already told you how he didn't like to get them dirty. There in the yard, among the piles of finished bricks, I turned toward him even though I was embarrassed that he'd see me naked and scold me for being shameless, but as I thought it over I decided that I didn't have anything to blush about, because indecency was really more about ugliness, and I wasn't skinny and I wasn't bloated like now, a bag full of fat with the fluids erupting out of me, no, I was a kid with good muscles shaped by the labor of hauling bags of cement to the mixer, pouring the mix into the molds, and working the handle of the brick press.

His blue eyes regarded me from under his bushy eyebrows as he turned his hooked nose and sharp chin toward me, bent by his years, nodding like a night bird hunting for seeds in the dark. He kept his hands in the pockets of his blue nylon jacket and his Yankees cap pulled down to his ears, big pink ones bent double because of their size. "Baseball is your destiny, boy, a great destiny," he said by way of introduction, with a friendly smile that I didn't expect. Then he came a few steps closer and threw his arm around my shoulders, naked as I was. I felt his cold, bony hand on my sweating skin covered with the same cement dust that was caught all the time in my hair. "Why? Don't ask me, that's just how it is. But if you really want to know, I'll tell you you've got long arms that make for a good *swing*, you've got eyes like a cat, and you've got hidden power that can clear fences, that'll show itself if you eat well, if you eat eggs, milk, oats, and red meat. You want to know something? When Yogi Berra asked me why I was so sure he'd be a great catcher, I told him to stop asking me dumb questions, anyone could tell his body was made for handling pitches, like some crouching idol you might see."

Once Casey Stengel appeared to me, I knew my destiny was to bring glory to Nicaragua with a bat in my hands, that people would remember me, that they'd remember how every time I stood in the batter's box, dreams would take flight in the stands like doves popping from a magician's hat, fans would be on their feet by the thousands, hoarse from cheering me as I circled the diamond after each *cuadrangular.* A great reporter, Edgard Tijerino Mantilla, wrote that my name belongs to history. My feats are told in all the files full of clippings, photos, and certificates that I've got piled right here, next to the altar, because when I lost my house in the barrio of Altagracia the only things I could save were my papers and two of my trophies, the ones right next to the boxes of files. The gilded trophy that looks like a Greek temple held up by four columns, that's for winning the batting championship in the World Series of December 1972, played here in Managua, the series when I hit the *jonrón* that hung the Cuban team, invincible up till then, right out to dry.

That series, our Nicaraguan all-star team is staying in the Gran Hotel, and I'm already in bed because we've got practice early the next morning, but someone starts banging very assertively on the door to my room, the night after we beat Cuba, and my heart is in my mouth but I go open up and there's General Somoza in person, with all his entourage, I can see men in suits and officers in military caps behind him, so I rush back to wrap myself in the sheet because just like with Casey Stengel, the time he appeared to me, I'm naked as the day I was born, and in stomps Somoza and behind him the television crew with all their lights, and he sits down on my bed, tells me to get comfortable at his side, the cameras focus on just the two of us, me wrapped in the sheet like the statue of Rubén Darío in Central Park, him in a linen dress shirt and smoking a big cigar, and in front of the cameras he says, "What would you like? Ask me for anything." So after a lot of hard thinking and dry swallows, while he waits patiently, a smile on his face, I say, "General Somoza, I'd like a house."

That prefab house, two stories, a *living* and a *porche*, it was just about ready, only waiting for them to run the electric lines in one of those new neighborhoods that didn't collapse in the earthquake that practically leveled Managua that December. I went to look at it a bunch of times, the house of my dreams, and they promised me I'd get it right away, but it all dissolved with the excuse that the earthquake had left a lot people homeless, people needier than me. A whole year went by, a lot of petitions and pleas that got me nowhere, but then the fans, still so grateful even though they were busted flat because of the earthquake, made contributions to a fund set up by *La Prensa* to give me my house. Some of them gave money, some came up with zinc panels for the roof, others with cement blocks, and in my files I've got the picture from the paper where the publisher, Dr. Pedro Joaquín Chamorro, is giving me the keys. But that's the house I lost because a half-sister on my father's side, a loan shark by trade, whom I left in charge of it when I had to go live in Honduras because after the earthquake nobody could devote their attention to baseball, she sold it without my permission, claiming that she'd lent me money. She swindled me, and I was back with no roof over my head again.

About two years ago I went to the Sports Institute to try and get work, and after I haunted the place for quite a while they finally agreed to my idea of letting me work with little league teams, because even if I couldn't get out of my chair I could still coach the kids, tell them how to grip the bat the right way, how to get set on your legs while you wait for the pitch, how to extend your arms when you swing, but then what they paid me was a joke, the checks always came late, they made me come in person to cash them, and with all those humiliations, I quit. Anyway what good was a meager salary that wouldn't even cover the cost of my medicines? I'm a walking drugstore, remember, and Doña Carmen, Lord Jesus bless her, has a terrible time getting me the medications I need the most from the charity hospitals, pastor as I am of a very poor church in a barrio where the people live in puny shacks under the blinding sun between garbage dumps and ditches of dirty water, shacks made mostly of scrap, using rocks to hold down the zinc roofs because they don't have nails, making walls out of black plastic on one side because they don't have wood, and a cardboard refrigerator carton on the other. So how are my flock going to have money for my medicines if they have to struggle just to get enough to eat, and it's not just that, because as their pastor I hear all the problems they bring to me, shut in here the way I am, I hear about drug addicts who beat their mothers without pity, girls drawn into prostitution at thirteen, liquor stores that open at dawn, and I offer them divine solace, but I know that it takes a lot more than preaching the Word to tamp down evil when there's so much crime and so many needs—and yet they keep saying we had a revolution here.

My house in Altagracia was worth everything to me because it was a gift from my nation of fans. I had the uniforms I wore on my different teams in a special glass display case, along with the one from the national team with "Nicaragua" in blue letters and number 37 on the back, a number that if we really respected national treasures would have been retired so no one else could use it, and my bats, including the one that hit the home run off of Cuba, my glove, my medals, relics that one day should go into a hall of fame. But my sister the usurer wasn't satisfied just to sell the house to a pool hall owner, she also took my mementos for herself, or she destroyed them, I never found out which. If I still have the boxes of files and the two trophies, that's only thanks to a brother of mine—one who later lost his legs in an auto accident—who sneaked into the house before that leper sold it, and he rescued them.

When the war to get rid of Somoza broke out in 1979, I was a truck driver. It hadn't been easy, but I had managed to buy a truck on credit, and I was doing all right hauling watermelons and tomatoes to Costa Rica, but when the fighting got roughest by the southern border I hid my truck for a few weeks hoping that the situation would improve. Then on the day of the triumph I got caught up in the explosion of joy and I put the truck at the service of the guerrillas pouring into Managua, to bring their troops to the plaza for the celebration. I made at least five trips, buying the fuel out of my own pocket, and look what happened next, some troublemaker from my neighborhood accuses me of being a Somoza paramilitary and right there in the plaza they confiscate my truck, and all my appeals to get it back are in vain, they can't prove I was a paramilitary, which is ridiculous, but they tell me look, we found this photo of you with Somoza, and it's the picture of the night he surprised me in my room at the Gran Hotel to give me whatever I wanted as a reward, a false promise, as I said, but that's it, case closed, so I try to go to the truck dealership to explain but they won't back down, a debt is a debt they say, they unleash their pack of lawyers on me, if you don't pay you're going to jail for fraud, so suddenly I find myself a fugitive, first my truck is stolen in broad daylight, then the mockery of having to flee from the law, that's the prize the revolution gave me for hitting in fifteen straight games in the World Series of '72, a record that nobody has been able to take from me, this is the *comandantes'* praise for the four triple crowns in my untarnished career. You can see that the fame Casey Stengel promised me that moonlit night was no guarantee against injustice.

If I hadn't been a ballplayer I would have liked to be doctor, a surgeon, but poverty buried that dream, and instead I had to do all kinds of jobs from the time I was a kid—baker's helper, auto shop worker, machine operator in the Santiago brick factory. "Don't worry about it," Casey Stengel told me when he appeared, "Back in Kansas City, I wanted to be a dentist but my family was as poor as yours and I could never achieve that goal, and anyway I wouldn't have been any good at pulling rotten teeth." I struggled to study at night and graduate from elementary school, at least, while I worked days in the brick factory and they gave me a place to sleep, and after the apparition, though I wasn't earning much, I took charge of my fate and saved part of my pay to buy my equipment, the *spikes*, the bat, the glove, though it meant I had only one Sunday shirt, not to mention a lot of other sacrifices I made. "Baseball is something sacred," Casey Stengel told me, "and it's a lot like a hermit's life. Look, your neighbor Don Nicolás was right, my boy Don Larsen threw a perfect game though he was far from perfect, because he thinks he's such a pretty boy he's always been more interested in a wild night on the town than a good day on the mound. Let me tell you this in confidence, my boy: that perfect game of his was a fluke, and my prediction is that in a few years it will be forgotten. True glory is about perseverance, and when you win it, you have to give up the vices: liquor, cigarettes, gambling, and especially women, because all that is a ball of wax that brings you to the brink of poverty. Fame brings money, but there's nothing worse than becoming famous and then being out on the goddamn street." And look what a prophecy that was, because everything I earned I spent on women.

Did I already say I've got ten children spread around, each with a different mother, because in my time of fame and glory I had no shortage of women? After a good day at the plate they'd come up to me wherever they caught sight of me and whisper in my ear, like maybe we'd be dancing and the whisper would go, "I'm not wearing a thing under this dress, put your hand here on my miniskirt so you'll see I'm not lying," these are memories I try to keep under wraps now, in my role as a pastor, and I regret that I couldn't ever take Casey Stengel's advice. However flattering those memories can be when they make themselves at home in my brain without my permission, what good are they now if at almost sixty I suffer from heart inflammation, arthritis, hypertension, and above all obesity, so these visions of women become an awful torment, they must be my form of punishment, these memories of women of all sorts and sizes who offered themselves to me, like the one who owned a Mercedes Benz with seats that smelled of pure leather, or another who invited me to her seaside mansion in Casares, or the one with pale blue eyes who sold beauty products door-to-door out of a suitcase, the one married to a fancy lawyer who took poison on account of me and nearly died, or finally the young student, graduate of a typing school, who asked me to check her out while we danced and sure enough she wasn't wearing anything underneath.

After they confiscated my truck I was really feeling helpless until some Pentecostal brothers started coming by every day, bringing me illustrated pamphlets with full-color photos of happy families, where the husband in overalls is up on a ladder cutting apples from trees loaded with fruit, the wife and kids in straw hats are in their own garden carrying baskets full of all kinds of other fruits and vegetables, and some white lambs with ribbons on their necks are grazing in a green field, all that under a shining sun that seems never to set, a portrait of the bliss that comes only with the infinite mercy of faith, according to the two brothers preaching in a real torrent of words, one brother from Puerto Rico and the other from Venezuela, the Lord doesn't care at all about worldly glory, or the traps of fame, they said, and they sat there for hours as if they had nothing else to do in the world but preach the word to me, as if I were the only one among so many suffering souls they had to convince, and then they gave me a Bible, and when they could see the fruit was ripe they told me which Sunday to come and be baptized.

For the ceremony they gave me an outfit like what they always wore, a white shirt with long sleeves, though I couldn't button the collar because I was too fat, and a black tie, they rented a pickup truck and lifted me into it chair and all, and in the truck bed with me came the preaching brothers and some guys with guitars who sang hymns of joy all the way to a quiet bend in the Tipitapa River shaded by a row of willow trees, out beyond the plywood factory, where the brothers lowered me, chair and all, into the water up to my head like it was the River Jordan, so even though I caught a chest cold with a cough that kept me up all night, I did feel a deep peace inside and was thankful that the Lord Jesus was in me. I have to admit I never thought I'd be a man of the Word, since what I knew how to do was hit *jonrones*, which doesn't require any eloquence at all, but the Holy Spirit took charge of my tongue and I learned to preach, which is why the brothers could trust me with the responsibility of this church before they departed for other lands.

If some baseball fan from the old days were to see me here, inside these four unfinished walls, under this zinc roof full of holes that let in both dust and rain, in this little church with its four rows of wooden plank benches and an altar with a red curtain that was once a campaign flag of the Liberal Party, my boxes of folders and my trophies in a corner, and the folding cot that Doña Carmen sets up for me every night, because the church is my home, that fan I'm talking about wouldn't believe I'm the same guy, especially if he understood the invalid's state I've fallen into, to the extreme that one night I defecated while I was sleeping, in a dream where I felt I was emptying my intestines without meaning to, and I've never felt greater pain in my life than to wake up smeared in my own excrement; that fan who once worshipped me would be tremendously disappointed, not to mention those women who took off their underclothes before coming up to me, the king of the *cuadrangulares*, so I could feel the smooth naked skin underneath their miniskirts.

What good was fame to me? What good did it do me to see

the world, to have my picture in papers that are now yellow with age inside my folders in cardboard boxes? I remember the night in January 1970 in the Quisqueya stadium in Santo Domingo, when it was my turn at bat and a band in the grandstand broke into a merengue because we were behind in the seventh inning and the people were dancing, screaming like maniacs, I had two *strikes* with a runner on second and all night long I hadn't been able to figure that pitcher out, a big black man, six feet tall, throwing fireballs one after another, but this time he tried to surprise me with an inside curve and I swung with all my might and watched the ball going high and higher out to deep centerfield, beyond the lights, beyond the starry night, dissolving into a cotton speck, a far-off feather, into nothing, and me just watching it go, not starting to run yet, not until it was completely lost to sight and then I let the bat fall like in slow motion and when I did start into my trot I doffed my cap to the stands in the half-light, the opposing fans who now formed a well of silence, so quiet I could hear the murmur of the sea as I circled the bases full of jubilation, down the third base line, now tingling with emotion, and when I crossed *home plate* dazzled by the glow of the flashbulbs popping, I felt like crying because that swing had turned the game around, and we won it, and now it's not that night in Santo Domingo but the December afternoon in '72 when we beat Cuba thanks again to my four-bagger, for which they promised me the house they never gave me, and now the sound of the sea is the voices of fans who stand and scream, on and on, from the seats, rowdier and rowdier as their emotions run high.

The Lord Jesus has set things in front of me: life and death, good and evil, because the Word is very close to me, in my mouth and my heart, for me to fulfill; so I accept that I shouldn't complain or succumb to regrets. In the solitude of this church over which the wind shakes and shudders, rattling the corrugated zinc roof, I sit on my wooden chair and I know that when the door opens by itself with a creak of its rusty hinges, and the figure of Casey Stengel appears backlit by the noonday glare, with that face like a bird dipping down after seeds, and he says to me, “Are you ready, son?” it will be time to follow him.

THE END OF THE GAME

Carmen Hernández Peña
(Cuba)

Carmen Hernández Peña (Ciego de Ávila, 1953) is a poet, fiction writer, playwright, and literary critic. Besides her twelve book-length works in these genres published in Cuba, her poetry has appeared in anthologies and periodicals in Colombia, Brazil, Puerto Rico, Mexico, Spain, and the United States. In Ciego de Ávila she has been editor of the magazine Fidelia and the publishing house Ediciones Ávila and the organizer of a series of poetry workshops and literary salons. She is also a dealer in rare and used books and spent three years as a street vendor of Styrofoam witches.

Dear Pablo, Claudio left. All of sudden he said he didn't love me anymore, and he left. Who can I talk to other than you? I'm feeling a very sharp pain inside my chest. Claudio left and I don't think he's coming back.

Next day.

Pablo dearest, I think this is turning into a diary. Yesterday

I told you I had chest pains, precordial, I thought. But now I think it's just cartilage.

The son of a bitch did the right thing by leaving before I ended up throwing him out. Don't tell me this is just sour grapes. Not a bit. I want to go back to living the life I had before, without worries, free as the wind. I'm sick of men in their underwear (and you'll remember what our professor Rosario said about them).

It's been a while since a man fell in love with me. Jesus! Men give me a rash, they give me fits, drive me to drink, I don't know what. They're like vultures, is what they are.

Two days later. 10:30 at night.

I've been a modern Penelope, reviewing my list of suitors, and there's only one I like. He's been after me for some time. I know it. Everybody knows it. I haven't seen a sign of Claudio. They say he's going out with some other woman. Strange, no? Maybe he's a got a nickel-steel prick. To hell with him. I don't want him around me again. What a chameleon.

The one I like is called Esteban, and he looks like a Visigoth. I never saw a male Visigoth, but they must have looked like him. Maybe we knew each other in a previous life. Any minute, he'll grow tusks and assault me. Now I'm sleepy, it must be from this psychological vampirism. I hope I dream about him and not that lizard or oyster or whatever.

Next day. 5 p.m.

Pablo dearest, today I've worked like a dog. And I've made money, enough to buy an umbrella, but what's the point, better to buy chocolate cookies or a good moisturizing cream—it better be good, for the vampire bite. Everything reminds me of Claudio, even the umbrella. I saw him yesterday. When we started dating we went to a restaurant. It was cold and rainy, and he put on a shirt of mine that was a little tight on him. Me, my only white dress, the only dress I had back then that was good enough to go out in. God, we were happy. What I jerk I was. Yesterday I saw him, and he looked pretty good, although people tell me he's got a face like a cabbage. That's not me saying it. I'm out of my mind, a little. But I was talking with the Visigoth, who is quite shy. I don't like shy men, and it wouldn't be very elegant to fall in love with him. He asked about Claudio and I said that he split. When I wake up in the middle of the night it takes me a while to accept that Claudio isn't here. He was a Moby Dick in the bed, took up a ton of space. No way I can sleep in the middle now, I've got to squiggle off into a corner, like the whale might suddenly drop from the sky.

Two more days gone. 11:00 at night.

The Visigoth took me by the hand, and I felt a little jolt in my stomach. That's a good sign, the jolt, because it always happens when one falls in love.

I've read a few things, but here I'm trying to bring you up to date on my life without Claudio. I thought it would be worse.

Oh—I've got another one on the list. In hand, or better to say before my eyes. A guy I've known for years, a contemporary of mine, but he's kind of a ladies' man. He's spent his life getting married and divorced, although I don't want him as a husband, of course.

About the guy you know, the less said, the better.

The next day.

Pablo my very dearest, you called but I wasn't home. I felt so bad about it. You know, I've been thinking, and I believe I made a mistake. I've taken Claudio way too seriously, I mean, à la Sophocles, sometimes à la Shakespeare. Claudio is more a guy to be taken à la Moliere or maybe Hector Quintero. I won't deny he's a son of a bitch, a degenerate, a Rubik's cube, but not entirely. Anyway, it's too late. He's gone. I saw him yesterday, with his Mona Lisa smile. I've wasted a lot of time on anxiety and anger. And what's worse, sometimes I've forgotten I exist.

Two more days.

Pablo, my dear, it's not the Visigoth and it's not the ladies' man. It's the nomad. Because you can't deny that the most nomadic of all is a baseball player. Yes, a baseball player, what the hell, you don't have to get all surprised. It's a long story and, like always, it's got a tragic aura to it. Tragicomic, anyway.

It may surprise you that I'm fond of our national pastime, but it's true, I'm a fan. At the stadium I met a girl who's friends with all the players. The other night, after the game, she invited me to a disco-karaoke place to celebrate a win. It's been a while since I frequented places like that, and I was a little afraid, but I went.

And right there I started dancing with the *catcher* of my team. Baby, I need to explain to you, the *catcher* is the one who gets the ball, the receiver, the one behind the batter in front of the *umpire* (that's the guy everybody screams curses at). Anyway, we started dancing (he's a terrible dancer), and what can I say, I was in seventh heaven, because the guy is really good-looking (when the game is on TV, you can see him). He said he always saw me in the stands, he took special note of me, all the nonsense people say when they're dancing. From song to song and drink to drink, my *catcher* starting pulling me closer, and I went along. Dancing in the half-light, you know, and sometimes none at all. He invited me to his room and, tramp that I am, I went.

Well my boy, when we got there and he turned on the light, he recognized me. He said, "Hey, you're what's-her-name, I've seen you, you're a writer!" And I'm remembering the story about Virgilio Piñera and the mulatto (you remember? the longshoreman who wanted to talk about books?): "Get dressed and get out!" This fine man has been courting me with all kinds of silly shit and explaining how he locates his hand and his arm and his feet and even his ass when he's up at bat, when suddenly he gets all intimidated and the next thing I know he wants me to recite him a poem. Are you listening? A poem, at that of all moments? My god, this could only happen to me. And I'm going, No, my love, you talk, please, baby, I want you to talk, baseball is my favorite thing in the world, all the peaks and valleys I've lived through watching the games, so please, honey, talk to me about baseball, the bat, the mask, the umpires, sons of bitches that they are. But he's like, no, please (you see?, "please" and everything), you're such a cultured and literary woman (only it sounded more like "lititery"), why all this about baseball, I'm just a country hick, I need some polish for when I go abroad because, you know, baby, I'm going to be the best *catcher* in Cuba. And I'm like, okay, that's more like it, back to baseball, but he's no way, Barbarita—may I call you Barbarita?—I don't want to talk about that.

Now stop and consider, Pablo dearest, after ten or twelve glasses of rum, when one's body—especially my body, aching, bruised, trampled on—is ready for a good fuck, for a tremendous *body-to-body* with that guy built like a brick wall, along comes this crap about a poem and literature. No, honey, I don't have anything to recite, I can't even remember a poem, the only poem here tonight is you, your batting, the way you rob your opponents of hits. So in the face of all that, he started kissing me, which of course he does as well as he *catches*, but that's all it amounts to, because I've never been with a woman like you, my queen, and it's messing me up, I don't know how to say this nicely, pardon my language, but the horse won't move an inch. And I'm like, damn, because what I needed right at that moment was nothing more or less than a horse, a good one, a stallion, the *summum* of all stallions, the Trojan Horse, the cosmic one. But he was nearly dying of shame, Pablo my only, and so I consoled him, I said it doesn't matter, my stud, this can happen to anyone. He insisted on accompanying me home, and he made me promise to be in the stands that next day, in the same seat as always.

The worst part was that when he kissed me goodbye, the horse . . .

I'm saying, Pablo, that when my *catcher* and I said goodnight in front of my house, the horse said, here I am. What a waste, no?

That night I didn't sleep well. I dreamed of Claudio and of him. I got them mixed up. Him in my bed, Claudio playing baseball and hammering immense home runs that flew over the fence and kept going and going until the ball reached the moon or who knows where. For two days I didn't go to the stadium, because I was kind of embarrassed, so I listened to the games on the radio. The announcer just kept on repeating, "There's something wrong with our man behind the plate, he seems like he's got a cold or flu. . . . now he's touching his waist, maybe he's injured . . . ," but I knew the poor guy didn't have a cold and wasn't injured. It was because of the horse.

Finally, I went to a game and I sat where I always do. When they came out to warm up, he saw me and gave me a kind of shy wave at first, he put two fingers to his mouth like throwing me a kiss, then he threw me the ball, and luckily a couple of guys next to me reached out and one of them caught it, because otherwise it would have cracked open my skull.

The game began. That night they stole second base off him fourteen times, third base twice, and a very handsome shortstop stole *el home*. A total disaster, my friend. I felt like everyone knew I was responsible, though in fact it wasn't my fault at all, I was more the victim. When he came up to the plate, I don't even want to tell you, instead of keeping his eye on the ball, he turned his head to look at me. He got hit by two pitches, once in the back (of course, since he wasn't facing the pitcher) and once in the shoulder. The score was seven to four in favor of the other team, and I was furious, all I wanted to do was jump down on the field and shake him, thump him, do something.

Ninth inning, bottom of the ninth, that means it was our last chance. The first two batters went down—the first one struck out, the second hit a line drive to center that was caught. The next two got on, a walk and a hit batsman, and the one after that hit a *línea* to left that got down. So, bases loaded, Pablo my dearest, and it was his turn to bat. All thirty thousand people in the ballpark started booing him. The pitcher even made a special threatening gesture—I'm an expert in gestures—the jerk touched his own balls and then swiped the index finger of his right hand across his throat, which in baseball talk means, "I'm going to strike you out and I've got the balls to do it." My *catcher* was bouncing on his feet, he crossed himself, he looked my way. The pitcher wound up and threw—*strike* called, no swing. The pitcher wound up again—low and outside. One and one. Another pitch got by him, one and two. At that moment, Pablo my love, I remembered who I am. I stood up and yelled, "Rito, that can happen to anybody. You're the greatest, give it a whack." Pablo, it felt like a Kevin Costner movie. Me on my feet, the game down to the last strike, him batting, or trying to, which isn't the same, him turning toward me in slow motion, and then a big *close-up* of his face that said, "This *jonrón* is for you." The pitcher taunted him again, and this time it was my guy who touched his balls. I tossed my scarf and my beret on the field and the umpire yelled at me, "If you don't calm down I'm calling the police and having you arrested," so I made a dirty gesture at him. The pitcher got tired of this and threw one practically in the dirt, but even so my guy reached for it and made contact. Pablo, right from the start I knew it was gone. I think it hasn't landed yet.

So that was it, we won the game—remember, we had

three men on, the hit scored four runs, we won eight to seven. I launched myself onto the field and hugged my *catcher*, everyone congratulated him, and they tried to lift him up in the air. I said, "I'll wait for you to change," but just then who should appear but Claudio, with two policemen, saying I'd gone crazy because he walked out on me. I cursed both Claudio and the cops with such conviction and in such pure Spanish that one of them said, "between husband and wife, best get out of the way." Claudio asked me, "What the hell is going on between you and Rito?" And I answered, "What the hell is it to you?" But now Claudio had his arms around me and almost pulled me bodily out of the stadium. My *catcher* saw us from afar and started to laugh. He threw me a kiss. Since then I've only seen him on the field. They haven't stolen more bases off him, and he hasn't been hit by any more pitches. Probably someday he'll be in the World Classic or the Olympics.

THE LAST VOYAGE OF ARCAYA THE SHARK

Rodrigo Blanco Calderón
(Venezuela)

Rodrigo Blanco Calderón (Caracas, 1981) is the author of three collections of short stories: Una larga fila de hombres (2005), Los invencibles (2007), and Las rayas (2011). He is the founder of the publishing house and bookstore Lugar Común, and he teaches literature at the Universidad Central de Venezuela. At the 2007 Hay Festival, Bogotá, he was named as one of "Latin America's 39 Most Exciting Authors Under 39," and he was awarded a residency at the University of Iowa International Writing Program in 2013.

National tragedies put a country's great truths to the test. What happened in the state of Vargas confirmed, among other things, that at least in Venezuela there's no more odious character type than the one that appears when somebody takes on the persona of a diehard baseball fan.

I already knew this, but the tragedy unleashed by the December rains of 1999, during the key month of the Winter League pennant race, had momentarily clouded that truth.

That same tragedy, in its context of death and defenselessness, would soon bring it back to mind because of a thoughtless joke made by a coworker of mine.

One week earlier, at the outset of the disaster, there had been a national referendum to approve or reject the new constitution. On the day of his victory, even before his celebration of the result, the president expressed his solidarity with the people of Vargas. The celebration of the new Magna Carta would be introspective and discreet because the rain, though so far only a mournful drizzle, had already brought the first fatalities. Perhaps the president had an intuition that history, when all is said and done, repeats itself. Or perhaps he sensed that pure willpower and an inclination for theatrics can compel it to repeat. However that was, his moderation in victory succumbed to a terrible onset of last-minute pride—the same pride that brought Odysseus to shipwreck long ago and now would impel several thousands of people to shipwrecks of their own. Just when a fair wind was blowing the end of his speech toward a safe harbor, the president decided to recall the impious and outlandish words of Simón Bolívar, pronounced on March 26, 1812, after the historic earthquake that shook Caracas: "If Nature turns against us, we will fight her and make her obey!"

The night following that day of December 15, 1999, the tragedy unfolded. A week later, when the approximate count of those dead and disappeared in the mudslides of Vargas had exceeded the ten thousand mark, I left my desk in the newsroom and went out into the hallway for a smoke. My idea was to make both the cigarette and the walk last as long as possible. This showed me I wasn't cut out to be a reporter. Not only was I exhausted, but I was taking after the weather, my heart a darkened sun of melancholy and depression. I didn't have the strange sense of strength that journalists feel when contemplating the misfortunes of others amidst the frenetic activity of colleagues. I didn't feel that my interminable and uninterrupted hours of work at a small desk in the newsroom were helping in any way.

I took a few puffs and saw Carlos come out after me. His face, like everyone's, looked agitated, feverish. We exchanged silent glances. I don't know what he might have seen in my eyes, but for some reason he tried to cut through the moment's tension with a joke. And before my eyes, Carlos stopped being Carlos and turned into an imbecile.

"Now it's true for sure," he said with a feigned grimace. "The Sharks are down to their last few fans. Just Juan Pedro and you, and the five poor souls who'll be left in La Guaira after the flood."

He gave me an awful slap on the shoulder to help me digest his comment, and he left. I stood alone in the hallway, quizzically regarding the extinguished end of my cigarette. I lit it again, and while exhaling the smoke I remembered some lines of poetry I'd memorized long ago.

> "King" is another word for tyrant
> East, west, south, or north—
> And one of the worst among them
> Is Spain's Carlos the Fourth.

That verse comes from the local anthem of Vargas. I discovered it by accident in an illustrated geography book when I was a teenager and Vargas was still just a municipality of Caracas, not yet a separate state. The lines and the pictures fascinated me because they were so full of anger and violence, the seed of a furious revolt against power, the song of a guerrilla movement. I memorized them so as to reaffirm, both to myself and to my family, that my having been born in La Guaira, Vargas's capital, was not an accident but rather the hand of fate.

All this began a little earlier, when I was about ten or eleven and had started to cultivate a rather ostentatious

"Guairismo." My family was full of followers of Caracas and Magallanes, so to declare myself an inveterate Sharks fan was the first act of conscious independence I can recall. Both Caracas and La Guaira played their home games at the University Stadium in Caracas, so to attend only the La Guaira games was a declaration of principle. To memorize Vargas's anticolonial anthem was—to judge from the puzzled expressions of my parents, siblings, and aunts and uncles—an act bordering on extremism and delirium. Many years had to pass before life taught me that my passion for these stanzas was not just a whim. What taught me this was not only Carlos's cruel joke, but also my long conversation with Juan Pedro the next month, which is really the subject of this story.

By January of 2000 the die was cast. The country was drenched and desolated, Vargas had become the new Atlantis, and the Sharks were facing up to yet another defeat. The Sharks had a new manager—Luis Salazar, one of the emblematic players of the victorious 1980s—but he failed to lead them to what La Guaira's fans and players had by now come to see as utopia, which was to make it to the second round of the playoffs. The year before, Pedro Padrón Panza—the team's father, owner, and founder—had been carried off by the slow river of time. As if his death were not enough, among those who had now disappeared in the mudslides were his son and successor Peruchito and Peruchito's own son, the tiny grandson of the founder. La Guaira's Sharks had been stripped of past, present, and future. Those three deaths were the definition of orphanhood, the birth certificate of a ghost team, a team doomed to swim in the waters of nostalgia and sadness in search of its lost origins. These were the kinds of thoughts that drew me farther down the hallway on that Monday in January, or maybe those thoughts were, like me, dragged down the hallway by the smoke of the cigarette. Down the hall I went, and down the steps, and out onto the street.

Now what? I could fulfill some commitment elsewhere in

the city, I could go home, or—if it wasn't yet time to go home and I didn't have any pressing errand—I could go have coffee at La Sociedad, a friendly dive on the same block as the paper, the kind of place where a pair of ancient but still powerful speakers broadcast *vallenato* hits morning, noon, and night. There I headed, and on the way I set to work reviewing my list of frustrated loves. There's nothing strange about this. It goes right along with misspending endless hours bemoaning the bad luck of my baseball team. All La Guaira fans see our club's fortunes as a coded but shared version of our life stories. Each of us deciphers the code differently.

Lists of frustrated loves are so long they'd be endless if the minor detail of death didn't get in the way. Sometimes that process works backward: people die because they can't remember who they love. People whom accident or illnesses turn into vegetables, in a state of living death, are unaware of the world and have forgotten all their loved ones. They're exiled from life because they can't participate in love. I suffer from a humiliatingly similar but opposite malady: I fall in love at least once a day. For me, it's impossible to see a beautiful or mysterious woman on the street and meekly accept that I won't get to know her. I console myself by recalling that neither requited love nor loyalty changes the picture very much. I've spent nights lying awake beside a body that I love, one that sleeps trustingly by my side, when I still don't fully understand what it's doing there, how it came to be given to me. My list of frustrated loves is long because every love, in the end, is a frustrated one.

Let me say that my tailspin into memories that particular morning had a more concrete cause, too. Because of the rain and pressures of work, my friend Daniel and I had not been able to repeat the trip to the Paraguaná Peninsula that we'd made in the first week of January the year before. This meant Daniel would have to wait for Carnival time, or maybe Easter, to visit his family; it meant I had to wait indefinitely to revisit the scene of a lovely memory. The beaches of Adícora and Buchuaco would have to get on without us, as if our feet had never touched their sands. They would become an empty photo album, all their images erased.

• • •

At first, when I saw her approaching the waterline, I tried to rid myself of deceptions. I told myself that what I felt was a symptom of my incurable belief that nothing in life is an accident and that first encounters are really the repetitions of earlier contacts that pass unrecognized.

I remember that her feet had just entered the water, that she did not recoil, and that at this moment she let down her hair. With this image going right to my heart, I decided to send all my reasonable arguments back to Caracas without me. I felt that I knew her and that our meeting was no accident, or that accidental meetings are really dates made in dreams that we forget when we awake.

Late in the afternoon, when the group she came with began to pack up their things, I gathered the nerve to speak to her. Taking advantage of her last plunge into the warm waters of Buchuaco, I approached her just as she was emerging from the sea. In the gentle breakers, I pretended to be washing the sand from my feet.

"I recognize you," I said.

She stopped in her tracks, a bit surprised. She gathered some locks of hair and secured them behind her ear.

"Where from?" She showed no sign of being offended.

"I don't know."

"You don't?"

"No. But I'm sure I know you. Are you from around here?"

"From Buchuaco? No, I'm not. I'm from Judibana."

I found her precise answer both amusing and admirable. As if she were saying that being born on the same peninsula was a pointless abstraction, a generalization that did no justice to her home town.

"And your name?" I asked.

She hesitated a few seconds. I think my interrogation was starting to strike her as strange. I looked her directly in the eyes, without blinking, as if a break in eye contact would snap the slender thread of our communication.

"Irene," she said at last.

"Irene from Judibana," I whispered. "A lovely name."

Irene seemed to like this. She asked whether I still couldn't remember where we met.

"Still a blank. Probably I'll remember too late, when I'm on my way home."

"Aha, you're from Caracas?"

"No," I said, and this answer was heartfelt. "I'm from La Guaira." And then, without knowing why, I added, "It's too bad I know I'll never see you again."

"I don't get it. You remember me, but you don't know where from. You meet me now and you're sure we'll never see each other again. Are you dreaming?" She ended with a smile and stepped forward out of the water.

"Maybe we're both dreaming."

Irene shrugged expressively. She seemed amused by the idea.

"I tell you what," I said. "In a few years, I'll write a book about you. A novel. If you read it and we see each other again, we'll know it wasn't a dream."

"And how will I recognize the book?" she asked. She raised one hand to her forehead to shade her eyes from the sun sinking behind me.

"By the title. It will be called *The Man Who Talked About Irene from Judibana*. How does that sound?

"Strange," she said. "But I like it." And she left.

• • •

When I reached La Sociedad, I felt so downcast that I got a really pathetic idea. I would drink steadily the rest of the morning and all afternoon. With any luck my boss would find me there and fire me on the spot for being completely drunk on a workday. That idea faded when I saw Juan Pedro at one of the tables near the back.

I didn't know him very well. We'd conversed only once, in a superficial way, although about subjects of some depth. This was at the German embassy on the way out of a talk about Thomas Mann that I'd attended more out of snobbery than true interest. I knew Juan Pedro worked in the literary section, and he knew that I was a newcomer assigned to sports. I still had that conversation fresh in my mind. I remembered that he said reading Mann had been the second most important moment of his spiritual life. Although he had no biblical beard, nor did he dress in black or wear a *yarmulke*, Juan Pedro told me he considered himself deeply Jewish. As far as I understood, there really was a far-off Jewish ancestor on his mother's side of the family, but the heritage had been abandoned for generations until he, as a teenager, started to turn the pages of the Old Testament and found himself trapped in the Book of Job. Job's story amazed him because of the way it took the most demanding human experience of all—faith—to its outer limits.

"Faith only makes any real sense," he said, "when you have nothing left to believe in."

This conviction, which like the universe stemmed from the creative force of the word, acquired new dimensions from the hypnotizing power of other words, other reading. When Juan Pedro read *Joseph and His Brothers*, he started to feel a deep antipathy toward his own name. The four volumes of Mann's monumental work made him regard his apostolic name as an error committed in excess. He told this to his father, who heaved an exasperated sigh and told him to stop reading so much, to look for some distraction that would take him away from books.

"Books are for reading, son," he said. "Not for acting out."

Juan Pedro answered, with encyclopedic precision, that he was sure he'd read that same statement in a Mafalda comic. His father told him to go to hell.

If you ask me, Juan Pedro's father was right. Juan Pedro's Judaism was an accident of reading converted to destiny. Soon after I sat down at his table in La Sociedad, he provided further evidence. Out of courtesy he asked me how I was. I told him that I was feeling sufficiently sad, nostalgic, and spiteful to get drunk at eleven in the morning in the bar closest to my job. Juan Pedro took this seriously and, making a gesture of disgust, told me that on the contrary he would not touch a drop of alcohol for years to come.

"I was up all night reading a book of stories called *The Invincibles*, and believe me, by this morning I was plastered. I've never seen so much drinking in a single book in my life. So let's just have coffee or juice, okay?"

We ordered two big mugs of coffee with milk and two bottles of mineral water, and then we continued talking. Out of both politeness and curiosity, I asked him about the state of his faith. He gave me a stiff look, the coffee mug suspended in his hand. Then he dropped his eyes to the floor in silence, as if my question were a confirmation of something he'd been thinking.

"Stronger than ever, it seems today," he said with complete seriousness and a grimace suggesting distaste.

"Why? What's happened?"

"What's happened?" he said opening his eyes wide. "Does everything that's happened seem like nothing to you?"

When I answered, half confused and half embarrassed, that I didn't know what specifically he meant, he recalled that aside from that conversation in the German embassy, we had never talked.

"Strange," he said suddenly, unable to hide a sudden blush. "For a moment I had the feeling we were good friends. Old acquaintances, from long ago."

Then, as if trying to make up for the slip, he told me his life story, the crucial turning points in his personal pilgrimage that the morning's news of the death of Leonel Arcaya had thrown into stark relief.

The last thing I would have expected from someone like Juan Pedro was for him to be a baseball fan—much less an inveterate follower of La Guaira's Sharks. Only then, when he began to sketch the outline of his story, did I remember my "accidental" encounter with Carlos, whose cruel joke about the Sharks, Juan Pedro, and me flashed in my memory like a forgotten jewel in the bottom of a bag, the symbol of a bond that already linked Juan Pedro and me long before we met.

After telling his son to go to hell, Juan Pedro's father feared that his offspring could end up plunging his head into the toilet bowl or, worse, into the polluted currents of the Guaira River. Deciding to put his own advice into practice, one day in October of 1986 he took the boy to the University Stadium to see a game between the Caracas Lions and the Mariners of Magallanes. The experience proved disappointing—a small, unenthusiastic crowd and not much in the way of passion on the field. This was because, at least in the '80s, the true rivalry in Venezuelan baseball, the most heated and infectious, was between the Lions and the Sharks. Despite Juan Pedro's lack of enthusiasm, the father persevered in taking him back to the stadium, this time to watch a game between Caracas and La Guaira.

After that, everything changed.

"In those days," Juan Pedro recalled, "every spectator who entered the stadium got a small lottery ticket. You scraped the card and the name of a player appeared. If the player on your card scored the first run of the game, you automatically won a prize. A prize that equally automatically, at least for me, became a physical and unforgettable reminder of that game."

Juan Pedro's card bore the name of Leonel Arcaya, a player unknown either to him or to his father, an expert on the Venezuelan League. A player about whom it is almost impossible to find any information today. Arcaya was a backup second baseman for the Sharks in the era of the famous "Guerrillas," a nickname proclaiming their refusal to ever give up.

"The first run of the game," Juan Pedro said, "was scored by Arcaya. Between the halves of the seventh inning I went to the booth to get my prize." So saying, he put a hand into one of his outside jacket pockets, pulled out an old baseball, and rolled it across the table into my hands. I could just make out a scribble in blue and black ink, nearly lost in the yellowed leather. I assumed it must be Arcaya's autograph.

But this was not the end of Juan Pedro's connection to Arcaya. Years later, in the 1990–91 season, or maybe it was '91–92, a second magical event linked Arcaya, the history of our storied team, and Juan Pedro's own fate as a Sharks fan and a Jew.

It was a game against the Eagles of Zulia in which La Guaira was fighting for a spot in the playoffs. From the outset, things began to come apart. Eight runs by the opposing team in the first inning seemed to have sentenced the Sharks' dreams to death, a death already foreshadowed by the black bands around the right arms of all the La Guaira players in a sign of mourning for Leonel Arcaya's father, who had died a few days before.

In spite of the lopsided beginning, the game grew tense, with the atmosphere of a storm that has gathered but not yet broken out. The Eagles did not score any more runs, while the Sharks, as in a dream with multiple segments, began to close the gap little by little.

“In the bottom of the ninth,” Juan Pedro said, “the miracle occurred.”

With the score tied eight to eight, the inning began well, but then, in one of the unexpected shifts common in baseball, the going got rough. The Sharks opened the frame with a pair of singles, putting men on first and second with none out. As might be expected, the next batter was told to bunt. He bunted too hard, and the pitcher got the force at second. That left runners at the corners and the awful possibility of a double play that would keep the Eagles in the game. The next batter struck out on three pitches. All seemed lost.

Then came Leonel Arcaya’s turn at bat.

Ignoring a take sign, Arcaya swung at the first pitch, a changeup. He grounded weakly to second, evidently a routine play. Then at the last second, as in a story from the Arabian Nights, the impossible occurred.

“Just before the ball went into the fielder’s glove,” Juan Pedro recounted, “it took a sudden hop. It shot up like a firecracker and handcuffed the second baseman. It kept going into right field, and the Sharks were in the playoffs.”

“On the way out,” he added, “people talked about that lucky hop, how it must have glanced off a pebble, but I saw how Arcaya raised his arms to heaven, thanking his father for his decisive influence on the game.”

Time went by, and the figure of Leonel Arcaya disappeared peacefully in the unfolding of new games and days and other names that far surpassed his. In the years that followed, Juan Pedro’s attention shifted from the individual magic of Arcaya, which only he could see, to the new shadow that gathered around the team.

The 1993–94 season marked the beginning of the end. La Guaira plunged into an unthinkable losing streak of fourteen straight games, a new record. At the end of the season, Luis Salazar announced his retirement, which was the confirmation that the fearful Guerrillas of the ’80s had surrendered their arms. The next year there were casualties both on the field and in the stands. On April 28, shortstop Gustavo Polidor died under a hail of bullets in a robbery attempt. In October, José Ignacio Cabrujas, the country's most incisive intellectual, died of a heart attack while his final article was still ringing in readers' ears. The article was in the form of a letter addressed "Dear Padrón Panza," in which Cabrujas apologized for having tried to shift his loyalty to other teams and requested—in what turned out to be his last wish—to be readmitted to the files of the Sharks.

Juan Pedro felt that this string of events was not just a run of bad luck. The team's drop into the cellar of the standings, its years without making the playoffs, the deaths that depleted the history of the franchise—these were all indications of a greater collapse. What happened on the field proved to be a prefiguration of the debacle that would engulf the state of Vargas at the end the decade. To Juan Pedro it was evident that the Sharks and La Guaira, the team and the city, the fans and the inhabitants, had been chosen for this suffering by God or fate. What happened in December 1999 was the full reverberation, in the sphere of reality, of what had been building up in the baseball league.

This equation led Juan Pedro, in turn, to a bizarre theory about the relationship between devotion to La Guaira's Sharks and to Judaism, or at least the arbitrary version of Judaism that he had minted for himself. He was sure that a follower of La Guaira, especially one who lived or wanted to continue living in what remained of the state of Vargas, constituted the tropical, Venezuelan incarnation of a Jew—a Jew, he said "in the true sense of the word." I never quite understood this true sense, but I can cite the strange example that Juan Pedro himself put forward that afternoon over coffee in La Sociedad.

"Imagine Job, on the edge of madness, when he had used up all his rage and despair, trying to soften the bitterness of his defeat by getting roaring drunk and dancing the samba on the stage of his own destroyed life."

The famous samba dancers of La Guaira, who still today enliven the right field stands of the stadium, became, for Juan Pedro, the celebrants of a macabre spectacle. Their festive and militant rhythm, which persists imperturbably in the face of what happens year after year on the playing field, fascinated him in an uncanny way.

"The samba has become our emblem," he said. "No one can understand how the worst team in the league has the most enthusiastic fans. They don't understand this irrational joy, resistant to failure and death. They don't understand that this is all the team has left."

During our conversation in La Sociedad, I couldn't grasp the full reach of Juan Pedro's outlandish theories. However, as the years have gone by I've seen the abysses that his words anticipated. In November of 2004 our Sharks—managed by the former Caracas infielder Jesús Alfaro—broke their infamous 1994 record by suffering fifteen consecutive defeats. In January 2006 we were hit by the death, from a mysterious illness, of Carlos "Café" Martínez, the most beloved, problematic, and inimitable player the team ever had. Our past was now dead, and our future as shriveled as a dried-up riverbed. Today, January 1, 2007, the date on which I am composing this chronicle of despair, that baseball drought persists like the negative image of the deluge and slides.

Off the field, the reality is not very different. Years after the tragedy, the state of Vargas remains devastated. During the Carnival of 2005, a new flood drowned the scarce hopes that had flowered, more from inertia than activity, in the ruined areas. In March 2006 the viaduct connecting Caracas and La Guaira collapsed, rendering the state of Vargas a forgotten peninsula. The inhabitants' response has been resignation. The majority have adapted to living among mud, rocks, and the vestiges of what they once were. As a people, they have turned their territory into a great edifice of grandstands, where they get drunk and sing, with crazy abandon, the song that relieves their distress.

Toward the end of our conversation, Juan Pedro remembered that I still had the baseball in my hands. He asked for it, and I rolled it gently across the table. He held the ball tightly, as if in proof of the solidity of memory.

The news had come to him that morning on the radio, and it had left him hurt and perplexed. Like everyone, he had already known of other similar cases reported in the previous days. The dimensions of the tragedy were reflected in the enormous distances that many bodies had traveled because of the force of the landslides. Corpses of people who were pushed into the sea along the coast of La Guaira appeared weeks later, hundreds of kilometers away, on the beaches of Morrocoy.

To learn that Leonel Arcaya had met a similar fate broke Juan Pedro's heart. Arcaya's body had been tossed indifferently by nature, the way a hopeless shipwreck victim tosses a bottle into the sea.

However, Juan Pedro said, his face twisted in confusion, Arcaya's death had a peculiarity that neither religion nor fandom could explain. Unlike the other bodies, Arcaya's corpse had not come to rest on the Morrocoy coast. Instead, like a solitary fish, it had continued its journey westward to the warm shores of Paraguaná.

"No one can explain how his corpse managed to get that far," Jean Pedro said, squeezing the baseball between his hands.

"Where did they find it?"

"In Buchuaco. I think that's just before Adícora," Jean Pedro said.

When he said that, my heart sank too.

By the time we parted, it was already late. Juan Pedro walked out with his gaze lost in space, the mystery surrounding the last voyage of Leonel Arcaya accentuating his pain.

I couldn't say a word. I was speechless. I had no way to explain to him that Buchuaco, with its waters warmed by love and courage, is the place where the dreams of a shark go to die.

THE STADIUM

Arturo Arango
(Cuba)

Arturo Arango (Manzanillo, 1955), is a fiction writer, essayist, screenwriter, and dramatist. His publications include the novels Una lección de anatomía, El libro de la realidad, and Muerte de nadie; the story collections La vida es una semana, La Habana elegante, and Vimos arder un árbol; and the stories "En la hoja de un árbol" and "El cuerno de la abundancia." Three of his stories have been adapted as feature films, for which he wrote the screenplays. Vagoneros, a film about the underworld of the Mexico City metro system, based on Arango's original screenplay, is scheduled for release in 2017.

In the stadium, under the stands, there's a small counter selling only cigarettes, cigars, and matches. Its glass display case forms a horseshoe in front of the main stairway leading up to the stands, so everybody at the ballpark goes by sometime during the two hours that a baseball game usually lasts. Yet the counter's limited offerings condemn it to be just that, a place that fans pass by.

The individual in charge of this tobacco stall was a man a little past fifty who had been there forever. Four days a week during the long series of playoffs, there he would be—friendly to whoever stopped to buy anything, always alone behind the counter, apparently sleeping in his seat while everyone else's attention was glued to what happened on the field.

This man liked baseball. More than that, baseball had been the passion of his youth. To baseball he had devoted his most enduring dreams, and he gave up on making it all the way to the major leagues only when he realized that he was smaller and weaker than most of the other boys who, like himself, dedicated their afternoons to knocking the stuffing out of the horsehide in the neighborhood sandlot. Later he understood that he was also not among the speediest, nor did he have anything like the quickest reactions, so little by little as the years went on and he was no longer in his teens, nor even a young man, his aspirations faded away.

Of all the necessary traits to succeed in baseball, he knew that he possessed only two: persistence and faith. Yet armed with these two, even after the age of twenty, while others gave up their passion for the game to devote themselves to activities closer to their daily lives, he still believed he might come to don a flannel uniform and *spikes* and play on a real field instead of the stony patch of ground that had left eternal impressions on his knees. This almost came about. He knew the game well enough and his arm was good enough to get him added to the roster of a local team, chosen to play right field. But that was the final dream of his youth. Life proved more recalcitrant than he thought when his father, grown too old for all the responsibilities of his several small businesses, decided that the son needed to take charge of the bodega. This did not require a great effort: the small storeroom and set of shelves that had been his earliest childhood kingdom occupied the corner part of the family's large wooden house.

Therefore when—many years after the day on which he

had to return the uniform bearing the number 4 (his personal choice) and the *spikes* he had barely gotten to wear—he was offered the job of running a concession stand at the brand new stadium, he felt he had received a small, late, but still tangible compensation for his unfulfilled dream. In its own way, that niche allowed him to be part of a true ballpark such as he had never imagined, a great monument of steel and concrete capable of holding thirty thousand spectators intent on what was happening on the perfect expanse of grass, gleamingly unreal beneath the mercury lights.

So now he was a piece of the stadium, a living one, somehow indispensable. Yet he was set apart from the game itself, the tension of the players and the crowd. He remained down below, alone, watching people go up and down the stairs that were his only link to the field. Sure, he got to be friends with ballplayers, managers, and umpires. They stopped to chat with him, to tell him about the game, how well or badly they'd done, the injustices of which they were victims, and he could measure the glory achieved by those men in terms of how many boys gathered admiringly around them, touching the fielders' gloves, the catcher's mask, which here, up close, became real.

But then he'd be plunged back into solitude, a solitude in the midst of thousands. So, alone, leaning on the glass counter, the man discovered that something more, besides the stairway, connected him to the field. A baseball game became, for him, a succession of sounds to discover and identify. He learned to separate one from another and to distinguish infinite variations. For example: a dry, metallic sound of bat meeting ball followed by a brief, explosive cry from the crowd could signify a hit with no men on base. (Although, in fact, only he would be capable of saying whether this is the correct way to put this example. We are only speculating, because there are so many similar sounds of bat meeting ball, and the enormous chorus in the stands has innumerable ways of responding.) At first, to check his impressions, he relied on fans coming down the stairs. “Was that a hit?” he would ask the first to appear after the crack of the bat and the resulting cheer. “Tagged out at second?” he asked the grimacing fan who appeared after a disapproving murmur swept the stadium.

After two or three years those sounds held few mysteries for him. His impatience at being stuck in the bowels of the stadium, subject to reactions that the luck or skill or will-power of others provoked in the spectators, began to vanish once he found another way to be part of the game. His observations became so subtle that fans on their way to the bathroom or to buy candy for their children were not surprised when this old man, who seemed to be asleep on his stool, would remark to them on events in the game that seemed knowable only by those occupying the grandstand.

This, however, was only a first step. It’s true that from this beginning he was able to extract more than a few nuggets of advice to offer the oldest of his grandchildren when that boy began to give baseball the attention it deserved, as he liked to put it. But later—one or two years before the youth reached the championship series as a player himself—the man began to realize that he had discovered only a very small part of what the stadium had to offer.

He found the first correlation almost by accident. Those who complained with unusual aggressiveness about a lack of matches on his shelves were actually upset by something more important: the home team was getting crushed. For two days he stoically bore the indignation of his customers, but on the third day, finding himself more annoyed than was advisable for his age, he decided to navigate his way through a labyrinth of work shifts and delivery trucks and so managed to get his supplies completely in order for the weekend. But his regular customers hardly noticed the difference, so ecstatic were they with the whipping their team was giving the opponent at the top of the standings.

The old man didn't really take it seriously. Just for his own entertainment, because he found the succession of cheers and silences that afternoon so uniform, so boring, he began turning over in his mind the idea of a link between the match supply and the fate of the home team.

After this rather foolish and innocent thought took root, he learned once again that he was only discovering bits and pieces, dispersed signals, because the team soon went through a bad spell, seriously bad, even though his shelves remained impeccable. Therefore what he had at first taken on as a minor entertainment now became a challenge. He felt mocked by having been sent a signal so small and incorrect. Night after night, day after day, the old man devoted himself to observing more deeply just what went on in the closed universe that very few could ponder as he could, from a state of meditative calm.

First, as might be supposed, he sought exceptional events, visible shortages like the matches, but he soon noticed that this approach gave him only the broadest-brush sort of evidence. He had to give more credence to other, subtler signs.

That was when the word "universe" began echoing in his mind. If the stadium was a universe, he thought, none of its parts could be ignored or discarded. Only someone like himself, used to doing his job without the slightest effort (selling, after all, had been his only work for more than thirty years) and master of the sounds that caused the rest to worry or to jump with joy, could listen with enough rigor and passion to the life of the stadium. A blinking of the lights, the illness of an athlete, an unusually long line at the pizza counter, three scraps of paper thrown away by different people that rolled to the same step on the stairs, a noticeable drop in attendance for a particular game—nothing lacked importance, and the old man took all of it in.

I've said this wrong. He did not take in every occurrence, but rather the relationships among them. This old man was an exceptional being. He had an intuition, a sensibility, that could direct his focus to what some might call the primary relationships playing out before his eyes (or in his imagination, for we can't say yet which was the case). This particular focus was what allowed him to accomplish what he did without being stymied by the vast and ungraspable welter of details. Thus, what the stadium offered the old man were conclusions. He read the stadium, read the universe whose laws he had, for the moment, been able to unveil.

Being the master of such certainties was not easy. He had to hide his sorrow from those who, during the first half of the game, came down to stretch their legs in full expectation of the sterling performance the euphoric radio announcers had promised for the home team. Yet at times the old man felt that thousands of people already knew what he had discovered. A smile on the face of an out-of-towner, a forced greeting from one of the few friends who visited him—these seemed signs that the language he had mastered was shared.

Also, game after game, he came to know more and more about the network of gamblers occupying the lower layers of his universe. He discovered their signals, knew which ballplayers were linked to that business—more abhorrent to him than to anyone—and gloated at the frightened eyes of those who thought they'd been found out by someone who was only approaching to ask for the time. Although he was wise to the bets, the money changing hands, and even the faces of the ones controlling the operation versus those who were mere messengers and bodyguards, he decided not to expose them, because he considered it unjust to wield the advantage that chance or nature had given him. At the same time, he often felt haunted by the possibility that one of the gamblers knew his secret, had arrived at it by a path as unexpected as his, and would demand his secret collaboration in that dirty trade.

When the championship series ended, his team's hopes for victory had turned to disaster. Perhaps, now that we've reached the off-season that follows the finals, this is the moment to explain that the old man's life outside the one area we've been discussing was uneventful, peaceful, and ordinary. He had a hardworking, obedient wife, three children who gave him no special trouble, a house in good condition and secure. The one thing disturbing his domestic peace during these years was the idea that his grandson could soon join the team aspiring to the championship. Then for several months hundreds of thousands of people would be paying close attention to what the young man could do. They would come to the stadium to applaud him or to boo him, they would identify with him while seated in front of their television sets, they would argue on street corners about his successes and his future.

"He's the real thing," the man's friends declared, and he smiled back to hide the one true disturbance in his life. Because that next season, when his grandson did take the field for the home team, new possibilities loomed. If everything happened in accord with a certain order of relationships, wouldn't it be possible to govern this order, to bring human will to bear on it, his own will in fact?

That was much more difficult than everything he'd achieved so far. When the next season came, his first tests were very cautious. The only time he would disrupt the stadium's order was when he was quite sure an adverse result already awaited the team. Even then, there was always the danger posed by chance, the possibility of making things worse. Later he would have to admit to himself how childish these experiments were: hiding the milder cigarettes for a week, moving the garbage cans around. But sometimes, when the consequences turned out to be negative, they could lead him to regrets. It wasn't easy for him, when the game was over, to see his grandson go by with hanging head, ashamed of a pair of ridiculous strikeouts that would be the talk of the town tomorrow morning.

As the grandson's first championship series neared its end,

though, the man was surrounded by the euphoria of those entering the ballpark to watch their team play for the top spot. He could feel a sadness, a sense that things were not going well. "Hopeless," he concluded after a half hour of close attention to reading the stadium.

Indeed, the championship series came and went without the home team's improving what the press took to calling its "modest performance." The old man's grandson was no longer one of the "reliable future stars" who would change the club's often sorry fate. The man passed the following year sunk deeply into himself, which his family members attributed to the ravages of age. "He's not the same anymore," his wife would tell close friends who pointed out his prolonged silences and distracted responses, or the averted eyes of a man whose gaze had always been lively and piercing.

Those silences led him to some undeniable conclusions: the universe he had been allowed to enter could be altered, but although his job had at first helped by giving him space for isolated contemplation, now immobility kept him from doing what needed to be done. The keys to change that he sought did not lie on the shelves under his counter.

When the next championship began, he used the pretext that a sports stadium should not encourage the tobacco habit and so won a change in his hours: the tobacco counter would close once the game got under way. This left him free to work the grandstand, selling coffee from a thermos in little paper cups carried on his belt, touring the length and breadth of his universe. Only the field itself was off-limits. Some of the first games of the series showed unexpected shifts of momentum that made the authorities suspect that the gambling networks had acquired influence within certain teams. A fifteen-minute blackout caused by a cat interrupting the three-phase electrical current, the home-plate umpire doubling over with sudden cramps, a flood in the men's bathroom—all these were experiments conducted as steps toward the goal of imposing changes that were not transitory but transformations dictated by his own will.

Having gotten this far, how can the old man be blamed for the mistakes he made next? He'd achieved much more than he could have imagined in the earliest days when it was all a puzzle of sounds and guesses. Intuition has its limits, and when the man hit these barriers, instead of respecting them, he stopped paying attention to his main gift, stopped letting his intuition guide him. To feel oneself so close to grasping the totality of something tends to lead to impatience. It wore the old man down, and his response was to try to reason everything out, to establish rules that would allow him to see all the strings he aspired to pull.

Thus, he determined certain dualities of action. The first such polarity had to do with what we might call a functional approach to the stadium: On the one hand there were aspects that did not exist as pure necessities of the game, but rather were imposed by its condition of spectacle. Actions taken to affect these aspects reinforced the tendency a given game had shown so far. If, on the other hand, the changes affected the stadium's essence as a ball field (extra humidity in the dirt, the breaking open of one of the bases) then the game would take a drastic turn. Later, he found this polarity insufficient. It referred only to generalities, and here the old man could have spotted his error, because, contradictorily, he came up with new pair of principles still more abstract than the first: what was dry, powered-down, or slow versus what was damp, powered-up, or fast. But by this time the old man was finding it very difficult to feel sure he was in control of bringing adversity or fortune to the team.

One night the television cameras—and soon, the fifteen thousand people in attendance—spotted an enormous flame that flared up beyond the left field wall. A garbage can was on fire, and just as the firefighters arrived to put out the blaze, a long ball hit by the grandson with two men on base landed in this same zone—a home run when the team had been losing by a difference that seemed insurmountable. But then the wind rose suddenly, giving the fire unexpected strength and sending tongues of flame leaping up a light tower, so the lights had to be turned off until the fire was completely extinguished. Soon after play resumed, an apparently inoffensive *roletazo*, a double-play ball, in fact, slipped between the young man's legs. The old man felt that the boos raining down on the field were addressed to him, to his arrogance.

Would this be his last attempt? On the way home, the boy walked beside him, uniform and *spikes* hanging heavily about his neck, and the old man was on the point of asking his grandson's forgiveness and leaving him to his fate. Behind the grandfather and grandson the enormous monument of concrete and steel was sleeping. The old man turned several times to look back at it, as if now that silence could speak to him. His intuition had awoken again.

During the next game he carried out no experiments at all. While he moved up and down the aisles selling coffee, he tried not to think about what was happening but to feel it, instead. Thus, each of his future actions grew surer and more ambitious. Now the stadium itself commanded him to loosen the lug nuts on the back wheels of a bus in the parking lot, to cut the electrical lines to the radio booth, and to toss two dogs onto the field, stopping the game while the umpires made fools of themselves trying to catch the animals.

If at first the stadium authorities thought they were victims of mischance, by this point they were convinced that some group, no doubt for political reasons, was trying to sabotage the national sport. Knowing this full well, the old man was able to escape the notice of the plainclothes agents whose embroidered dress shirts made them stand out, in his eyes, just as much as his grandson's red uniform.

We must give him his due. The night of the bus accident, he lingered in the lobby of the hospital until he was sure the driver and five passengers were out of danger. Remorse made him wait three games (two of them home-team losses, but a prior lead allowed him that luxury) before placing a banana peel on the bathroom steps for the pitching coach to slip on. The stairs were steep, the coach was not young, and the broken thighbone would leave him with a limp for the rest of his days.

"Am I God?" the man asked himself each time he arrived at the still-empty stadium. "Am I what people expect a god to be?" he asked again as he observed the green grass of the field, the newly smoothed base paths, the overwhelming emptiness that made his responsibility weigh so heavily. "Only partly," he answered on the night the stadium gave him an unconditional order: "The team will win if your grandson sits out the final game." Nothing could be so easy for him to accomplish, or so unfair. The only way to escape the order was to prevent the game from happening at all, but action on that scale was beyond his power. He might as well try to stop the rain, or wars, or other catastrophes that dwarf by far what unfolds inside a stadium.

He forgot that what he was about to do went against his intuition (but we have already pointed out that intuition has its limits) and against the very laws he had discovered and learned to employ. The result was that the game began after the brief delay required to separate the man's corpse from the same wires that, months before, had carbonized a cat. Only the following day, at the funeral parlor, did the grandson learn that he belonged to a championship team. At that moment he had no taste for glory.

BRACES

Yolanda Arroyo Pizarro
(Puerto Rico)

Yolanda Arroyo Pizarro (Guaynabo, 1970) is a novelist, short story writer, essayist, and member of the Bogotá 39, "Latin America's 39 Most Exciting Authors Under 39," selected at the 2007 Hay Festival, Bogotá. Her stories and novels have been translated into English, Italian, French, German, and Hungarian. Her 2007 story collection Ojos de luna was named a book of the year by the magazine El nuevo día and won the national prize of the Instituto de Literatura Puertorriqueña. She is a founder of the interdisciplinary and interuniversity Department of Afro–Puerto Rican Studies and the Women of African Ancestry Project, and she writes frequently in the Puerto Rican press and her blog Boreales.

"Go to the park and get your brother. It's time for him to do his homework."

You listen to the statement that brooks no opposition. This is the tone your mother uses when she's giving orders. It's her defense against any trace of disagreement. You hate it most of all because at the age of ten you can't use that tone with anyone.

You hate going to the local baseball field, too. You hate it because the place is so rundown, practically abandoned, and because it seems more like a swamp of filthy, clinging mud than a real park for playing baseball. And you know the difference, because you've seen real ballparks on television. This one is nothing like those. Besides, there's no place to get out of the rain, and rain is almost constant. The kids at school say that's due to the song, "Because in Bayamón, man, it does nothin' but rain." This isn't Bayamón, you tell them all the time. The refrain doesn't say anything about Barrio Amelia, the crowded and steamy place where you live with your mother and your younger brother, Viti, between Bayamón and San Juan.

But, since you have to go to the park whether you like it or not, you take Viti's bike, which he left on the porch when he set out on foot. It's got shiny chrome and it's spotlessly clean. You figure he left it there to keep it from getting splattered with mud, so you smile and pedal off. You go by the vegetable stand that also sells squeeze tubes of sherbet and cups of *limbers*, creamy frozen treats in many flavors that help to keep the coastal heat at bay. The attendant, Antonio, always gives you special treatment, hiding your favorite flavor—coconut—from the other kids. Nobody calls him Antonio, but rather *Trifinguers* because he was born without two of the fingers on his right hand, or maybe he lost them in an accident. Antonio *Trifinguers* is very likeable. Sometimes he'll sing you the song that goes "eternamente, Yolanda," by Pablo Milanés.

Soon you're at the park. As soon as your brother sees it's you on his bike, he starts to make signs that you shouldn't pedal past the critical point where the swamp begins. You play dumb and plow the front wheel right into the first mound of mud, where you bring the no-longer-so-shiny vehicle to a stop. From second base, your brother makes some new gestures that mean you'll get what's coming to you as soon as the game is over. You yell that mama sent you to come get him. And that's when you see her for the first time.

Or for the second or third time, actually, because you realize that you've seen her before, passing your house with her grab bag of shoeshine equipment. She gives you an intense stare. Then she slams the next pitch for a home run.

Viti trots around to home plate, and she follows, two runs in. That ends the game, and your brother comes over and grabs the bike out of your hands. He tries to clean it off with the wet rag that his sweaty t-shirt has become, but no way. So he jumps on and rides away, leaving you in the park. The rest of the players gather up bats and gloves, laughing and making conversation about Roberto Clemente and other players in the big leagues. She's joking around with the boys who haven't left yet, and you notice that they call her Alex. At one point the freckled kid with the reddish Afro who is tying his shoes calls her Alexia, but she corrects him. "Alex," she insists, and she smiles at you. You smile back, showing just your upper teeth, because by now you've learned how to smile without showing the lower ones, hiding your braces and the gap. You cover all that with your lower lip, which is thicker to begin with. Now it sticks out even more, and you look like you're biting it.

"I've got my kit right here," she tells the freckled boy, who's now the only one left. "Those shoes are going to get ruined if you leave them all muddy like that." When she crouches down and starts to work, that's when it happens.

It happens, and it's the most confusing moment of your life. Because Alex or Alexia, in bending down, exposes part of her behind. Her pants give way and expose a little of her butt. Over her butt and the crack between its cheeks, which you can just see the very top of, she is wearing boy's underpants.

You've seen them on your brother when Mama lets you both play in the rain without shirts and pants, you in your panties with the embroidered hems and Viti in his Fruit of the Looms like in the TV commercial where the men dance dressed up as fruits. You're troubled. You've seen this same kind of underwear on Antonio *Trifinguers*, when he wriggles around and his pants slide down, or when he's left his fly undone and he asks you, politely and apologetically, to help him zip it, which he can't do by himself because of the two missing fingers.

The redhead thanks her, reminds her that the gang will play ball again tomorrow at nine, and takes off. Now it's just the two of you in the middle of a baseball field that's nothing but mud. Though a drizzle starts to fall, nobody moves. Then there's a flash of lightning, followed by a clap of thunder.

"Will you come to the barber shop with me?"

You nod in agreement and follow her. Before you get to the shop with its red and white spiral pole, she looks at your feet and asks whether your sneakers are Converse. You tell her they are, but add right away that they're used, that your neighbor gave them to you when her daughter outgrew them.

In the barber shop the girl with the boy's underpants sits down in the big chair. She pays her dollar and gets a trim of her short hair while you wait on the steps, playing with some fallen strands of hair and beard from previous customers. When she's done, she springs up from the chair and tickles your neck to announce that it's time to go. You jump up too. After a block the drizzle turns to heavy drops and then into transparent balls that burst against each indulgent face, hers and yours. The rain comes harder, and you feel the globes of water striking your body—head, arms, chest, thighs—like strange twinges in your heart, like uncertain musical notes bouncing off the puddles on the ground. The rain on your cheeks and forehead, rolling toward your mouth, makes your heart beat faster, suggesting bigger storms to come. A raindrop, an invitation. A raindrop, a shock. A raindrop, and this cloud spilling over is now blessed among all the creations of the planet. You find a corner where a tiny bit of zinc roofing extends just far enough to shelter two. While you wait for the deluge to pass, she sings "I drink rum and beer to ease the pain, 'cause in Bayamón, man, it does nothin' but rain."

The downpour intensifies. The drops lengthen, turn oblong. A gray curtain takes shape around you, like a wall of drenched flowers. Alexia takes a long look at you. "You're gap-toothed," she says, and you hurry to close your mouth, which means you stop drinking in the rain.

"Are you a girl or a boy?" you ask. She smiles while she puts down her box of shoeshine stuff.

"I'm a girl."

You touch her hair and exclaim, "But you keep it cut so short, and you wear boys' underwear."

Alex shrugs. "My aunt says I'm a very special girl."

"Don't you have a mother?" you ask. She says she doesn't. "Or a father?"

"He's in jail. People say he killed her, and that's why."

Without asking permission, you lift up her shirt and open her fly. There are the underpants again, white ones with the unmistakable band of elastic around the waist. She looks at the kinky curls of your hair gathered into two unruly braids.

"I want to kiss you," she announces against the din of another thunderclap. You're about to ask why when Alex answers the question. "To see what your braces taste like."

When you say yes, it's already after the fact. The girl in Fruit of the Looms has brought her mouth to rest on your lower lip, the thicker one. Then it moves to your upper teeth, the ones that stick out. Instinctively you want to hide them, but her tongue seeks them. She lingers over the spaces of your gap-toothed gums, the irregular surfaces that your braces seek to corral, and you find yourself returning the motion, your jaw working up and down as if nothing else in the world matters. You drink in the elixir of her juicy saliva. Your lips open and close as the neighborhood seems to turn its sodden back. The two of you press your mouths together in a new way of moving, the newest in the world.

Finally the rain slackens and you pull apart, suddenly visible, the weather no longer a willing accomplice. You resume your walk and, reaching your house, you open the door that creaks on its rusty hinges. She'll keep going, you know this because she's holding tight to her shoeshine box. From inside, without looking, your mother yells, "It's about time! Get in here!"

One last drop falls on your nose. The two of you smile.

"I'll see you tomorrow, Alex," you declare. You don't wait for an answer. You've used that tone, the particular inflection that forestalls any contradiction, the tone that brooks no opposition. The one that works for giving orders. You no longer detest it. You laugh heartily, gap-teeth exposed.

THE REAL THING

Alexis Gómez Rosa
(Dominican Republic)

Alexis Gómez Rosa, born in 1950, is the author of such emblematic works of contemporary Latin American poetry as Adagio cornuto (2000) and La tregua de los mamíferos (2005). He has published more than fifteen books of poetry, winning the poetry prizes of both the Casa de Teatro arts center in Santo Domingo and the Dominican Ministry of Culture. He has been a pioneer in bringing together eastern and western influences in the Dominican Republic, both through his 1977 exhibit of concrete or pattern poetry in the Casa de Teatro and through his 1985 book High Quality, Ltd, which made use of the Japanese haiku and tanka forms.

Like much Dominican fiction, this story is built around political personalities and events well known to Dominicans: the repressive dictatorship of Rafael Trujillo (1930–61); its replacement after Trujillo's assassination by a new constitution and the popularly elected reform administration of President Juan Bosch; the overthrow of the Bosch government in 1963 by a military junta led by Colonel Elías Wessin; the ejection of the junta in 1965 by a constitutionalist uprising with support from some left-leaning military officers who demanded Bosch's restoration;

and the subsequent military intervention by the United States. What followed was a United States–organized election that propelled into power Trujillo's former puppet president, Joaquín Balaguer, who then dominated Dominican politics, with varying programs, from 1966 until 1978 and again in later years. The story makes reference to a period of abortive revolutionary activity and government repression in the early years of Balaguer's regime, followed by a period of economic boom and corruption.

Empty baseball field
— A robin,
Hops along the bench

—JACK KEROUAC

You're the real thing, man, you made it. You've got a million dollar voice, you're the archetype, the example of a pro behind the mike. *Side by side*, in center field, the amazing Willie Mays. What a game—adjusting your intonation just the right amount, on you go—the second game, 1962 World Series, Marichal on the mound, he delivers, *strike one*. One and one now on Roger Maris, evening the count.

We were still in high school, the Boys' Normal School, caught between algebraic equations and the pressing slogans of politics. Mama called you "my precious," which was a sign of the protective shield she wove around you, but we were never jealous because in truth you were always the most vulnerable, your nose running day in and day out, your body offering shelter to every cold and flu. That's why she rocked you in her arms, coddled you in her lap, called you "precious," which made you grumble and pout, which only got you another batch of nicknames added to that. Being the last of the litter was both good and bad for you. You got butter on the bread, ice cream on a stick, popcorn in your pocket. But on the other hand you were the first to get called out if you wandered off first base. Mama didn't like to see you getting soaked in the rain like the rest, much less tagging along with us chasing pussy, lining up for a go at Lucrecia's honeycomb. I won't broadcast this, don't worry, but you grew up a virgin with your peepee uninitiated while you hoped someday to get beyond the hankie with which you cleaned up your poor substitute. Those were difficult times for our elders, with their heads full of dreams and worries, and in our world, too, things began to go downhill; the sweet turned sour for men and women and those who hoped to grow into that state.

Nobody paid much attention, but you had left the earth behind, with your six feet five inches that made kids ask, "How's the weather up there?" You laughed, but what you really wanted was to be the cleanup hitter for one of the local sugar mill teams, for the Central Río Haina or the Ingenio Porvenir. That was wishful thinking, nothing more, rubbing salt in your wounds because you knew full well you were in hock to a heart condition, my man, and where you could compete was in the elocution contests ("To be or not to be") organized by the National Sugar Council.

Microphone in hand, you could mimic the best of them, you could make Buck Canel, that *gaucho* from Argentina, sound like the Dominican street, so that nobody stirred from their seat, because "don't go away, this is just getting good." You could do Rafael Rubí, those magical swings of his narrative bat, *a tomar cidra, mi hermano*; "ain't the beer cold!"; *special, mamita, special*; a sizzling line drive to *el jardín derecho*, off the right field wall. How you could memorize so many baseball expressions and inflections, I don't know, but I do know how it happened, my man. All those years under Mama's thumb didn't go for nothing, years when you had no better escape from solitude than the play-by-play over the radio, without the fits and starts and shocks imposed by female company, always on the make but scared of their own shadows, women who were like, "If I met you before, I don't remember it," or like, "I want to know if you mean business," and meaning business meant shelling out for a wish list that was as long as Mama's string of rosary beads. I mean it, my man, I'm offering serious counsel. Better to keep on jerking off, that's a ticket to heaven, or at least it's putting on the television and putting hands to the task in front of *EXXXtreme: free adult channel*. But you were a good boy, dedicated to your homework, knowing credit comes where it's due, poised at the brink of surprise and astonishment, a back-country boy who didn't know that life is a stillbirth of passions that won't always lead to a pool of peaceful repose. Force X goes up against force Y, tossing men onto battlefields, bleeding, mutilated, in the name of fierce ideologies. And war broke out within the house. On one side the certainties of the elders, anchored in their religion, and on the other you raised the demands of the needy and the banner of utopia. And I watched. A difficult moment. Blood ran in the streets, and we saw drops staining the newspaper—because newspapers don't lie, do they?—to the south of the barbed wire and the crossroads of anonymous Dominican corpses. First came the dust storm, the leaf storm that was brewing. First the dust, the leaf-storm of the days, and then the North American fleet, and in the mouths of the retreating rebels the songs of Fernando Valadez, composed in his wheelchair, the monsters and monstrosities of his hyperbolic imagination.

The end approached, foreseeably. Those who shuddered under the bombs came back to the barrio if they were spared by God and the National Guard. If the war was a paragraph, what followed were sentences. The highest fly ball is just an out if it's caught. I mean, start over, but it's never over. I mean, make peace with the world, or call the game a tie, but it's not a game. I mean, facing bunts and *pitchouts* and ninety-six-mile-an hour heaters. I mean, waking up every morning on the knife edge of the Cold War and swallowing, every morning, a mouthful of fear.

I think I see you, but I think I don't. I think you're coming, or you will be, after the "bloodless revolution" of Balaguer (big fish in a small pond, stocked by the Marines), I think I see you going out into the yard, under the almond tree, in your cap made of a nylon stocking and your coke bottle glasses that lend credibility to all the statistics and records you recite.

I see you there, a guava branch in your left hand to serve as a microphone for your impeccable play by play, as you segue with millimetric precision from the commercials of the Gillette Cavalcade of Sports to the games of the Leones de Escogido, the Red Network of the Leones, red for their uniforms, that's all. You were a sight to be seen, a voice to be heard, how you harmonized time and space with incomparable grace. Cities and stadiums, the golden age and the modern game, players and fans. It never ceased to amaze me, how you could jump from New York to Santo Domingo, from the World Series to the city championships, blending the incidents of the game with the news off the teletype, the world on your table, turning turning turning. "In Liverpool, England, a shaggy-haired quartet is changing the world," turn turn, "No water, no power, Balaguer thinks he's the man of the hour," turn, "Martin Luther King assassinated, Che Guevara falls in Bolivia," turn, "and is reborn on all the T-shirts of summer, internationalizing his redemptive revolution." After that, other names pushed their way into the *lineup*, uniforms changed, so did sympathies and fanatics and fans, or maybe what happened was just that a new franchise got hold of all the dreams. We changed, too, our hairstyles and cosmetics, the country changed, it was transformed, and came the day when you added your repertoire to the programming of Radio Universal, number one on the dial. At noon, the comedian Tres Patines; at 12:30, Sports on the March with Tomás Troncoso; and at 1:00, the *Democratic Tribune* with its infallible signoff, "Till tomorrow, Dominicanos—God willing." Yes, you changed because it was a different country. Juan Bosch offered us three square meals, as the saying went, but he brought us Tres Patines. Still and all, he was the best we ever had. We could hear him on our way home from school, from radio to radio, house to house, never losing the thread of his direct and simple speech. This was a curfew worthy of the name, an obligatory hour in which I was no longer just the son of Gracita but a son of Machepa, as he called the common people, sweaty and sipping my lemonade as I listened to his words. Then, after that, you'd go out into the yard again, under the almond tree, and "Jim Lonborg winds up on the mound, here comes the pitch, Javier punches a short line drive between *right* and *center*, moving the runners up to second and third." I remember how old Chilito loved seeing your imagination take wing on the rolls of teletype you suffused with new life. From the big leagues, your team from New York: "Horace Clarke, second base, *Clarke en la segunda base*; Rubén Amaro, *siore stop*, *Amaro en el campo corto*; Joe Pepitone, center field, *Pepitone en el prado central*; Mickey Mantle, first base, *Mickey Mantle en la primera almohadilla*; Charley Smith, third base, *Smith en la esquina caliente*; Tom Tresh, left field, *patrullando el jardín izquierdo, Tom Tresh*; Jake Gibbs, catcher, *Gibbs en la receptoría*; *y lanzando los bultos postales*, hurling the bales of mail, the golden lefthander, *el zurdo de oro*, Whitey Ford, with his record of eleven wins, four losses, and an ERA of 2.52." You were like Jorgito Bournigal, the encyclopedia of baseball, as they used to say.

By 1970 life had changed from a phenomenal thing to a phenomenon, and a sinister one. To stick your head out the window or door was to risk getting tagged out, a tag out of nowhere, no way of knowing whose gloved hand fired the shot. Doors and windows closed. Eyes closed, mouths closed, nocturnal writing on the walls, these are scars, knife cuts, cries that no one utters out loud. Mangá was killed last night, did you hear? They killed Sergio Boca de Rueda, they killed Homero. Sergio, who used to play with us on the *pley* in Pidoca. A great second baseman, Sergio Big Mouth, with those lips like the cuff of your pants. Now he's a mound of dirt in the cemetery of Los Mina, pissed on by passersby. In a Dantesque spectacle, they took the leash off La Banda. In Los Mina, with its early morning shoppers, its butcher shops that open at dawn, they let La Banda loose in their *jeeps* to make themselves masters of the night and the town.

The day dawned red. The news piled up in letters, a bloody background blare of lamentation and despair. It was all I could do to make myself open the mailbox or pick up the phone. I knew that every piece of news I received was coating me in a plaster of horror and depression, a terrible quota of death. I'd recently left the *country* (*you know?*) with its dark burden of days and flowers, of returning to funeral parlors as soon as one left. Those were the days when I decided to hop across the Gulf, after the death of René del Risco, the poet of our era, December 1972. Though I was living in New York, my habits didn't change. I'd still peek out on the balcony after eating, without Tres Patines, Tomás Trancoso, or the *Tribuna Democratica* but with those voices still in my head, and they took me into the yard below the almond tree. "What brand of battery, Johnny?" to which Johnny replied, "*Ray-O-Vac es la pila, pídala*," and this pitch for Rayovac was the overture to the game from the big leagues, Billy Berroa at the mike, Juan Marichal, the Creature from the Black Lagoon, on the mound, and Maury Wills at the plate, his bat never leaving his shoulder, "*strike cantado,* strike called, struck him *auuuttt!*"

But from a distance, a new tune was being sung, a new country unfolding within the old, an immense cornucopia made of smaller bounties in smaller hands. Here a sergeant served as regent, there a priest grew fat off his fief, over there a politician—mythic and mimetic—handed out the goods.

You, on the other hand, opted for the taming of the word, for giving it polish by freeing it from its impoverished literal meaning, from its single-minded intent to communicate. This was the other side of the coin, or of life, and you devoted yourself to literature, to avant-garde verses that would never win you a girlfriend, poems sad as the last pastry on the tray. Even so, you went off to work on a path parallel with poetry. Mornings saw you depart in your khaki pants, your white shirt with epaulettes that made you look like an air force officer, your bottomless glasses and, in your right hand, the book of your conscience, the one that held the arsenal of quotations you deployed in the studio, "from Santo Domingo to the world," to protect yourself from the world, because there's nothing better than a pair of good quotations to wield against intolerance and abuse. Or so you thought. Some were drawn from Nietzsche or Cioran, others from the catechism of the nearsighted left. And amidst one or the other, more and more your radio reports cited José Martí, who unified them all. And Rodó and Henríquez Ureña, the late Latin American humanists who opened and closed your daily broadcast on the day of Crowley's kidnapping, when the gringo military attaché was snatched while his head was in the clouds of his polo game. Minutes before, from the mobile unit of Radio 1000 on Your Dial, I heard you report that the United Anti-Reelectionist Commando had claimed credit for the kidnapping, demanding the freedom of twenty political prisoners and a plane bound for Cuba. The way you ended, the roller-coaster tone of your paragraph, brought you close to the mastery of Pedro Pérez Vargas, with his grave intonation and guttural closing on the dot of the hour. The comparison didn't sit well with you, but you let me babble on a little. This was not like the parody of Balaguer we did the famous day in the previous year when he wiped the floor with Elías Wessin, calling the general an "impenitent conspirator," the same man who'd paved his way to power back in '65. Oh, how your voice rose and fell with the inflections typical of the president, floating into the rough, nasal tones of a repentant *bachata* singer. Everyone marveled and laughed, enjoyed and applauded, ensuring you entrance into the Broadcasting Hall of Fame in the heart of the barrio of Ciudad Nueva.

Unblemished admiration, it could be said, if it weren't for the grudge that Lieutenant Cepeda began to bear you, because he had taken note of your parodies and hit the roof. "For a lot less than this, some morning they'll go look for him and find his mouth full of flies," he sputtered once. After that, our sessions grew less frequent, farther apart in time and space until your body, practically unrecognizable, made the microphones of the island orbit around you, the editorials and headlines of the country's papers proclaim your name to the four winds, fulfilling your destiny. As it was written, because he who finds himself among the famous becomes famous too. Your track record, your pedigree, your file of commendations grew as you fed it through your pilgrimage from boulevard to plaza, back street to barracks—here, "live from the scene," was found the body of a burly dark-skinned man with three bullets in his chest. To see and report (because you saw everything) was a single act of indignation and pain, as if wringing out the news of your own misfortune. The corpse was in front of you, but you didn't realize that your own blood had just mingled with that of the dead body in a fateful outpouring of grievances. After that, the news stopped being news. The studio filled with shadows, and other voices imposed their cadences and vagaries on the willing microphones. Little by little, a silence of chloroform and antibiotics overcame you, driving you back into your childhood niche of Vaseline and nylon stockings, my man.

You had nobody left to protect you. Mama was gone, signed by the Dodgers as we used to say, or the Cubs or Cards, depending on the era. Chilito signed by the Dodgers as well. But no sooner had you died than I was compelled to revisit your outsized hits and the meteoric pitches that froze the batter in place. Like the legendary character that would suddenly slide into a corner or make sensational plays up against the vehicles, you became player, narrator, and commentator all at once. Without a doubt, you made the era. You branded it with your voice in a continuous, uninterrupted play by play. But back, back, way back your figure was still there, behind the big box of an old Telefunken, compulsively repeating, "Good evening, fans, a very good evening. The Gillette Cavalcade of Sports, from Yankee Stadium, home of the Manhattan Mules, offers you its most cordial greetings." And also back, back, way back, from inside the house with the yard and the almond tree, a high-pitched, dry voice can be heard. "That's all for today," it says in a tone of annoyance. "Time's up. That's all for today, dammit. Turn the radio off."

THE WALL

Leonardo Padura Fuentes
(Cuba)

Leonardo Padura (born Havana, 1955) worked as a screenwriter, journalist, and literary critic before gaining international renown for his series of detective novels featuring Havana homicide detective Lt. Mario Conde, winners of the Dashiell Hammett prize and other awards. His novel El hombre que amaba a los perros, a reconstruction of the lives of Leon Trotsky and his assassin, Ramón Mercader, has been translated into ten languages, including English, and has received prizes in Cuba, Italy, and France. He once told an interviewer, "Baseball is a sport in which, when nothing is going on, that's when the most important things are happening—and the same is often true of literature."

The boy looked to be about seven, maybe eight years old—and left-handed, just like the man. He caught the ball, trotted back to his right, threw it against the wall again at just the right angle to run after the rebound and snag it with an outstretched arm, almost at the last moment, like a shortstop pursuing an impossible *roletazo* headed straight through the gap. Again and again, with great seriousness, putting the ball in the same spot or sometimes farther away, making it even harder to grab on the final *bound*.

The man watched the boy, no longer thinking about how this was going to wear out his sneakers. Sometimes the man made mental bets (that one'll get by him!) or commended a skillful catch (that kid is good!). After more than half an hour of this routine, the boy was bathed in sweat but still looked strong and agile and ready to throw the rubber ball hard enough to knock over the brick wall. Now his throws made him run faster, stretch farther, and snag the ball just on the outer edge of the webbing of his glove, just before it got through for the *hit* that would keep rolling to the outer limits of his imagination.

The boy's cap was on the ground in the shade of a laurel tree, next to which his dog lay splayed out on the sidewalk, a black and white mutt with a short tail, stiff ears, and tired-looking eyes through which it regarded its owner, without lifting its head, only when the boy tried for an especially difficult catch or when the ball came close to the dog. The pair of them had all the time in the world. Their lack of concern about the clock was something the man had almost forgotten. This was what kept him glued to the window, a sense that the monotonous game engendered an emotion shared only among the three of them—the boy, the dog, and himself—with no need for any other players or spectators. The wall, the ball, the glove, and the three of them all knew what mattered about every play. They knew that an effort to catch the most distant grounder was as decisive as the final play of a championship game. Then it occurred to him that the boy must imagine himself another Germán Mesa, a player of today, while twenty years ago it would have been Tony González, the shortstop of the Havana Industriales squad of his own dreams and nightmares, when he, too, used to throw a ball against a wall like that one, catch it that way on the edge of the webbing, and dream that his catches won championships and his future would unfold on the baseball diamond, the be-all and end-all of life's aspirations. Fuck that, he thought. Over the last two seasons he hadn't even gone to a game.

When he realized how much time had passed since he'd last been to the stadium, he glanced at his watch and, without meaning to, stated the time out loud: ten after three. An hour and fifty minutes of the workday left, and his desk full of papers. Again he watched the boy, the path of the ball—this kid never gets tired!—the dog's eyes alert to danger, and another good grab. He walked away from the window. He quickly swept up the pricing charts, the forms to fill in, the accounts and balances of the Department, the Management, the Municipality, the Firm, the Committee of State, and the Council of Ministers. In contrast to his usually meticulous organization, he shoved them all into the desk drawer along with calculator, paperweights, pencils, pens, erasers, telephone directory, and the newest book on Economic Planning and Work Organization. He turned the key in the lock of the drawer and studied the empty desktop of his accounting aide, Jiménez, who at this moment was on his way to the bank. He felt a vague desire to write Jiménez a note that would tell him, once and for all, "You're the most abject"—was "abject" the best word to use?—"and conspiratorial person I've ever met, and from now on I forbid you come near me and speak in your gossipy old lady whisper, because your breath is so bad it makes me nauseous and because I don't want to know what the head of personnel has let slip about her latest romance, I don't want to know about the director's extra coffee ration, and I don't want to know the newly appointed economic director's secret pastimes either." There was always a newly appointed economic director. But this was not the way to write the note, he thought. Better to just say, "Jiménez, you bad-breathed, brown-nosing, gossipy, dumbass sonofabitch, I shit on your mother's memory. Don't ever speak to me again." Signed, Z for Zorro.

In the hallway he picked up his time card alongside the receptionist's desk. He gave it a glance but did not feel any pride in the entry times that varied only between 7:40 and 7:56 and the departures always after 5:30. A model worker, he thought, as he stuffed the card into his pants pocket.

"Going to the main office, huh?" Martha asked with a smile. The receptionist had turned down the volume of her radio so as to concentrate on the unusual move he was making with the time card.

"No," he answered, heading for the exit.

"What if somebody calls you, Chino?" she yelled after him.

He paused in the doorway. "Tell them I went to play ball." And out he stepped.

When he reached the sidewalk, he felt different, felt like breaking into a run, but he had learned to tame his best impulses, so he walked. When he reached the corner he felt himself breathing easier. There was the boy, still competing with the wall. So as not to frighten him, he approached slowly, as if noticing the game only now. The boy realized he had a spectator, and at first he made two or three easy throws, but as the intruder persisted in watching, having stopped walking to do nothing but watch, the boy began to make more and more difficult plays. The man stood alongside the dog under the laurel tree and watched from there.

One rebound turned out to be uncatchable. It escaped the boy's reach but the man managed to grab it. He threw it back with a smile. The boy's "thank you" was barely audible.

"Hey," he said. "Is this your dog?"

The boy looked him full in the face for the first time and nodded, confused.

"What's his name?"

"Nerón Fernández."

He managed to suppress a smile.

"Nerón Fernández, I like that name. Does he bite?"

He knelt down alongside the animal, which was still flat on the ground, panting with tranquil regularity.

"Well, when he's eating, yes, and also . . ." the boy started to explain, but he had already leaned closer to Fernández and, using the dog's whole name, was scratching its head. After a brief look, the dog rolled over and offered him its belly.

The boy had stopped playing and watched the scene while bouncing the ball on the ground. There was a thirty-year-old man dressed in a short-sleeved guayabera with three ballpoint pens and the earpiece of a pair of glasses sticking out of the pocket. Wearing well-ironed blue slacks and shiny dark loafers, kneeling on the sidewalk and stroking Nerón Fernández's dirty belly.

"I've been watching you play for a while," he said then. "Look, I work in that office, the one with the closed window, and I think you're going to be a very good ballplayer. You'd be great at *siort,* except how can you play infield if you're left-handed?"

"I don't want to play *siort,"* the boy said quickly and with apparent confidence. "I want to play *center* like Javier Méndez."

"Then you've got to practice *flais.* Can you make one-hand catches like Javier?"

The boy laughed and let the ball bounce a few times.

"I sure can. Look, I take off and then camp under the ball, waiting for it, right there, no problem, and when it comes down first I grab it and then I go like this with the glove, like I was trying to catch a bug, but with the ball right in there"—and he swung the glove down with a matador's grace.

"Not bad!" he said, smiling. "Who taught you that?"

The boy sighed in the face of the inevitable question.

"My cousin Gabriel. He plays in the youth league. He's going to get me a helmet so I can play for real."

"You know, I'd like to see you catch some *flais*, see whether you're as good with them as with the grounders."

The boy looked both ways, up and down the street, and resumed bouncing the ball up and down.

"Nobody else is showing up, and you need two for *flais*."

"You've got a problem there, I agree. I don't like to throw *flais* to myself, either."

"You play?" the boy asked, surprised, not bouncing the ball anymore. He studied the man but decided he didn't look like a ballplayer, not in those clothes, not with that mustache and the pale, soft skin that meant a lot of hours in the office.

He smiled at the boy's justifiable doubts.

"Kid," he said, "I was quite a player when I was eight or ten like you. And believe it or not, I had a dog just like this one. Well, not quite the same, because he wasn't black and white, but black and brown, and hardly any tail, and his name was Curripio, Curripio Rodríguez, but he was like this one because he came along with me when I played ball."

The boy smiled. He liked the part about the dog.

"And where's Curripio now?" he asked, coming closer to where the man was still patting the belly of Nerón Fernández.

"He died of old age. About ten years ago. But I took good care of him, I gave him baths. You don't give Nerón baths, do you? Look at my hand."

He showed him how his fingertips were turning a greasy black. The boy acted like he saw someone turning the corner.

"He doesn't like baths," he said categorically. "Neither do I."

"Well, that's how things go. I don't think Curripio liked it much himself."

"So why did you do it?"

He smiled, thinking that he ought to come up with a good answer. But only two occurred to him: because he felt like giving the dog baths, or because dogs needed to be washed.

"Well, that's a long story," he began, to gain time. "The

thing is, Curripio was in love, and I told him if he wanted girlfriends he had to be clean, so that's why he let me give him baths. This guy doesn't have a girlfriend?" He touched the animal's belly again.

"He does," the boy said with a smile, maybe smiling over the word he was about to say next. "Margarita has a *puder* that he's the boyfriend of. I watched him do it. Look, you can see how long and red his thing is."

"Some guy, Fernández," he replied, thinking that everyone was probably happy with this arrangement except Margarita, because the owners of poodles were not much inclined toward mutts like Nerón Fernández, especially dirty ones.

Then he left the dog alone and stood up. His feet and his hips ached from the length of time he'd been crouching down.

"Didn't you go to school today?"

The boy started bouncing the ball again, probably bored with the new direction of the conversation.

"This morning, yeah. No classes this afternoon because they're spraying the school because almost everybody has lice. Not me, though."

"Lucky for you. What grade are you in?"

"Third, and headed for fourth." He seemed confident about the promotion.

"What do you plan to study?"

"I want to be a baseball player and a engineer who designs color TVs," he said with his accustomed confidence. "As a ballplayer I'll get to travel abroad, and as a engineer I'll make a lot of money."

At first, he wanted to correct the boy's grammar, to tell him it was "an" engineer. Then he wanted to say that at that age he had harbored similar dreams, but the way the boy ended the comment was too ingenuous for correction or comment.

"So, why aren't you at work, up there?"

The counterattack surprised him.

"I don't know, I came out for some fresh air and to talk with you."

"My grandma says I shouldn't talk with strangers. And you're pretty strange."

"What seems strange about me?"

The boy stuck a finger in his nose and said, "I don't know. If I was as old as you I'd be out looking for a woman."

He smiled. "Hey, who taught you that?"

"Nobody," the boy answered, looking at the end of his finger to see what it had found. "I saw you up there in the window a while ago, and you looked bored. Were you?"

"I think so, yes. Look, if I play some ball with you maybe I won't be so bored. Want to practice some *flais*? I'll throw them pretty high, and we'll see if you can catch like Javier Méndez."

The boy put the ball in the glove and backed away as he saw him taking off his dress shirt. He gave him another look of some suspicion, because it didn't make sense, in his experience, that a strange, bored, man in a guayabera should decide to play catch in the street. Meanwhile, the man hung his dress shirt on the trunk of the laurel tree and tried to salvage the situation.

"When I was in the youth leagues I played *center* for my team, and they taught me to catch the kind of *flais* that wanted to take somebody's head off. Did your cousin teach you to do that?"

"Gabriel's a pitcher," the boy said, wielding his strictest logic.

"Listen," he said. "May I wear your cap? You're not going to wear it, right?"

The boy looked at him. All the suspicion aroused by that question swam in his eyes. He tried to see himself from outside, wondering whether he would lend his cap to a stranger. Probably not, probably he would have said no, if he'd dared, but then he would have ended up saying yes, as he'd ended up saying yes so many other times in his life.

"Why do you want it?"

He dropped his eyes to the cap that he was already holding in his hands. It was made of gray denim with a red visor. It had absorbed the dirt and sweat of many a baseball game. He had once had an almost identical cap, and when playing ball was the most important thing in his life, he had hardly ever taken it off. Really, he wouldn't have wanted to lend his hat to anyone, and this boy shouldn't either, he thought.

"Never mind, you wear it," and he tossed the cap to the boy, who caught it in the air, gave it a moment's glance, but didn't put it on.

"No, listen, I don't care." The boy stepped toward him. "Wear it if you want." And he proffered it. The man smiled, but decided not to take up the offer.

"By the way, you haven't told me your name."

"You didn't ask. Élmer," the boy said, and bounced the ball twice on the ground.

"That's a good name. Isn't it? Look, Élmer, if you want, I could hold the cap for you while you play against the wall. I'll stay here with Nerón. You play."

"Are you mad at me?"

"No, it's okay. It's just that it's pretty hot out." He sat on the grass, next to the dog. The boy looked at him as if he'd done something wrong, which he hadn't. With a nod, he invited the boy to sit down next to him. Élmer smiled a minute and then obeyed. Nerón, without fully getting up, wriggled over to lie next to his owner.

"You know something, Élmer? I mean, you don't know it, but you should. I wanted to be a ballplayer and an engineer too. But I'm not either one. When I finished high school, I didn't get into the engineering major I applied for, and meanwhile I'd given up baseball to get better grades so I could study engineering. I bet you don't understand a damn thing

I'm saying, and neither do I, I swear. Now I'm an economist, I'm not famous, and I live in a house that will fall down on me any minute. And I haven't been able to go to Australia, which was what I wanted most in the world after baseball and engineering. Well, they can stick Australia up their asses," he said, and got up. He took the guayabera off the tree and looked at the boy, who hadn't stopped looking at him. In Élmer's eyes he saw fear and confusion. He must be a very, very strange man.

"Don't worry, I'm more afraid than you are," he said while he buttoned up the shirt. "If I weren't afraid, I'd send everything to hell and I'd go I-don't-know-where to do I-don't-know-what. But that's the thing: I am afraid, and I don't know where to go or why. But keep practicing. Maybe you'll be a ballplayer and an engineer, both."

Élmer got up too and came over to him.

"Listen," he said. "Why did you get so mad? Just because of the cap?"

"No, forget it," he said and took the cap which the boy was still holding in his hands. "You don't have any reason to lend me the cap. But I want to ask you something. Have you read a book by Jules Verne called *The Mysterious Continent*?"

The boy smiled and shook his head.

"It's an amazing book. It's about Australia, and when you read it you really want to go there. So listen to me. If you run into the book somewhere, don't read it, even if your life depends on it. Okay?"

Élmer lowered his eyes and then said, "You really are strange."

"Okay, I'm going. Take your cap. It was a pleasure to talk with you, Élmer."

He walked slowly toward the corner while wiping the sweat from his brow. As he entered the building the receptionist made a face at him and turned up the volume on her radio.

He returned his time card to the metal slot next to the clock. He climbed the stairs and thought he had never felt so defeated. He opened his office door, went in, and sat behind his desk. Under the glass top of the desk he could see the photograph in which he was smiling in between his wife and his son, Élmer. He also looked at the certificate citing the 120 hours of voluntary work performed by Élmer Santana, but he covered the photo up with the papers, forms, and brochures he took out of his drawer. Then he was sorry to have lied to the other Élmer. He should have told him that he'd studied economics because there was a directive from above that laid out the country's need for people to study that field, and he hadn't had the courage to say no, good student that he was; it was his duty as a young communist. He should have told him that he gave up baseball because he was a leader in high school, because he attended all the activities, all the meetings, all the study groups, so he didn't win a spot among the twenty-five ballplayers from his province to the National Youth League, and he lied to himself that, after all, baseball wasn't so important. But the fact was, as his father always told him, he had always been conscientious, and he could be proud of that. . . . Proud of what?

He left the papers on his desk and stood up. Those papers were the result of his conscientiousness. The air conditioning had dried his sweat. From Jiménez's bottom drawer he grabbed one of the cigarettes his subordinate hid there so as to avoid the requests of coworkers who wanted to bum one. He lit the cigarette and stepped over to the window. Élmer and Nerón Fernández were gone, leaving the street empty in the afternoon heat. The marks made by the ball were still visible on the wall, and by the laurel tree he saw a piece of gray and red cloth and wondered why the boy had left his cap behind. He never would have done such a thing. Without a cap he couldn't feel like a baseball player. He thought he ought to go down and get it, wait for Élmer to come back, give him the cap, and then tell him the truth. He ground the cigarette out against the floor and went down the steps again, at full speed. He had to recover the cap. Maybe this young Élmer would get a chance to go to Australia someday.

WINNERS AND LOSERS

Nan Chevalier
(Dominican Republic)

Nan Chevalier was born in Puerto Plata, Dominican Republic, in 1965. His published works are Las formas que retornan (poems, 1998), Ave de mal agüero (poems, 2003), La segunda señal (stories, 2003), Ciudad de mis ruinas (novel, 2007), Antihéroes onettianos: Habitantes de proyectos fallidos (literary criticism, 2012), El muñeco de trapos (stories, 2012), El hombre que parecía esconderse (novel, 2014), La recámara aislante del tiempo (stories, 2014), El domador de fieras (flash fiction stories, 2014), and Viaje sin retorno desde un puerto fantasma (novel, 2015).

> But all that's long gone now, all gone in the whirlwind,
> swept up like litter from the street, and what I've got
> left is the fat, just the fat because my muscles went slack
> and soft and I'm saddled with this useless reservoir
> that's slowly wearing me down.
>
> —SERGIO RAMÍREZ, "APPARITION IN THE BRICK FACTORY"

I was trying to find the men's room in a bar where I'd never been before when, suddenly, a lone man dressed in black caught my eye. This happened on a Monday when I'd gotten my monthly paycheck and had to rush out to watch the game and place my customary bets.

I've loved baseball since I was a kid, though I never really had an aptitude for the game. Now I think I know why: I tend to analyze what's going on around me too much, while sports (with the exception of chess) depend more on reflexes than reasoning.

I should make clear that there was a time when I didn't frequent betting parlors because I thought this violated the principles of sportsmanship, but poverty gradually lay siege to me and turned me from a loyal follower of events of muscle and mind to an inveterate bettor in places of diversion.

This time, after paying off my month's debts, I had a small cash surplus. My plan for the evening was to stay home, watch my usual police drama, and then make my bets over the phone while following the one big league game on TV. But just as Inspector Morse was catching the evening's murderer, the electricity went off, which sent me fleeing from the suddenly dark and stifling apartment.

It was already 8:02. The game would start in five minutes or less. Too late to get to my usual parlor, quite far from my neighborhood, selected so that no one would know the state of my finances. Instead, I drove just about a mile and parked in front of a little joint whose sign announced it as The Sporting Life. Underneath, a message in cursive letters urged, "Try your luck." The dark, tinted windows suggested rainy winter nights, while the pulsing sound of merengue and the tattered exterior told me the place would be a dump. "Typical barrio betting bar, full of criminals and delinquents," my deductive powers said. But I went in anyway and soon discovered my error, because I felt a homey atmosphere among the customers. I guessed that they constituted a sort of family that was more intimate than the crowd at my usual haunt in a much better heeled part of town. This was a family that assembled every night to watch baseball and other sports for the purpose of trying their luck while talking of many things under the magical effect of alcohol.

The room was larger than I had thought. Eyes on the TV screens, bottles in hand, fans hurried to place their bets. A minority of the customers were seated around some tables.

Impelled by the detective temperament that has always limited my full enjoyment of the best moments, I studied the furnishings and the staff: six flat screens, a slot machine with burned-out lights, a number of mirrors that multiplied us all into clones, a brunette waitress and a blonde one, and the barman, who also ran the cash register. Inspired by the waitresses' short-shorts (a rare sight where I live), I ordered myself a vodka.

That night's game was a makeup for one suspended fifteen days earlier on account of rain, the St. Louis Cardinals versus the Atlanta Braves. Since St. Louis was nine games up in the standings of the National League's Central Division, Albert Pujols had the night off. I didn't waste any time. I placed my bets and got ready to watch the game.

That was when, while searching for the bathroom, I saw a lone man dressed all in black. He was off by himself in a corner of the room. As if he suffered from some nervous tic, every twenty or thirty seconds he leaned over and, with his right hand extended, lifted the cuff of his left pants leg and stroked a metal object that seemed to be tied under his knee. I understood, with some fear, why the two waitresses were treating him with the respect and distance usually accorded to the dangerous or the terminally ill. The dim light in that part of the room (the man had apparently ordered the bulb above him turned off) made it hard to identify the object he was fingering, but you didn't have to be Kojak to deduce that this character had a weapon with which to protect himself from the probable criminals who visited this place. Or to commit crimes himself—who knew?—because these neighborhoods are unpredictable that way.

Through the multiple reflections of the mirrors I could see that alongside my table an old man was talking with a young one in a checkered shirt. They had a bottle of whiskey and were signaling the girls to turn down the volume on a thumping hiphop-mambo by Omega.

The customers applauded or cursed every play of the game. So far, both teams were fielding impeccably, and Tony La Russa was displaying his usual tactical skill.

I pretended not to be concerned about the man in black in the far corner. I subtly tilted my chair so as to keep his metallic object in view and, with one eye here and the other there, I also kept watch on the two nearby men whom the mirrors displayed deep in conversation.

At the feet of the old man, resting on a piece of cardboard, lay a small, battered suitcase or briefcase that he was careful to keep always in sight. Why did he need a briefcase in a place like that? Just as Inspector Morse would do, I made an association between the likely contents of the case and the suspicious attitude of the lone man in black with a nervous tic. Surely what was inside the case was money, and what was hidden under the cuff was a firearm or a knife. An assailant was among us, waiting for the moment to carry out his crime. The old man seated near me was going to be attacked by the enigmatic character in the far corner, who now, with some effort, stood up with his back to the room, facing the slot machine. But what if I were going to be the object of his attack, robbed of the few pesos I had left? I considered leaving, but I wanted to see how the game and my bets turned out.

Over the next few minutes four or five more men came in. From the greetings they offered I could see they were customers who lived nearby, not intruders from other neighborhoods like myself. Some of them greeted the old man warmly, and they seemed to be asking the brunette something about the solitary man. This made me feel a little better. Finally, I managed to stop worrying about the individual who kept putting his hand under the cuff of his pants. "What are you anyway, a policeman?" I asked myself, adjusting my chair more comfortably so as to enjoy the baseball game. "Did you come here to carry out a criminal investigation, or to try your luck in The Sporting Life?"

I ordered a second drink. A stranger in the place, with no one to talk to, I let myself eavesdrop on the conversation of the old man and the younger one accompanying him while on the center screen I watched my beloved Cardinals taking on the Braves. My team was winning, but the one I bet on was losing. Because how could I bet on St. Louis when Pujols was out of the lineup? But do you think that was easy for me?

While the commercials were on, the old man raised his voice so it carried over the chorus of other voices singing, "If you love me, why don't you call?"

"I wanted my boy to be like El Mamaguaia," he said, his gaze lost in the night invisible through the windows. I wanted to know what might lie behind that phrase pronounced in such a hopeless tone. I moved my chair closer to the old man and the young one in the checkered shirt, who was listening quietly while nodding slowly as if in agreement. "Not like Sammy Sosa or Manny Ramírez, you know?" the old man continued with his glass not quite grazing his lips. "I wanted my boy to be like the Mamaguaia of '98, that powerful, natural slugger that nobody would mess with. Ah, and as smart as the Alou brothers, you know?"

The solitary man in the corner signaled to the blonde, who attended to him immediately. He looked uncomfortable, as if annoyed that the old man had been raising his voice. He handed the girl a slip of paper, which she folded in two and secreted inside her top.

On the center screen, the game was half over, the Braves

now leading two to one in the bottom of the fifth. Without Pujols in the lineup, the Cardinals had no way to come back, I assured myself. Finally I'd make some money. Finally I wouldn't have to start the week borrowing money from the Brits in my middle-class neighborhood. I crossed my fingers and prayed for God to support the Braves.

Buoyed by my second vodka and the promising shorts of the waitresses, I came to the conclusion that luck would indeed be with me, that I'd be receiving money any minute. Whenever I drink, I feel happiness is just around the corner, and I let my imagination run away with me. My mind was wandering, and so were my eyes. I checked out all the screens while waiting for the old man to pick up the thread of what he'd been saying. On one of them, Andy Roddick had Roger Federer on the run in center court at Wimbledon; on the screen to its left, Holyfield was unloading hooks and jabs on Mike Tyson's face in the rerun of an old boxing match; next to that, a group of cyclists began a new stage of the Tour de France; then there was a local horse race: Psychotic the winner again, by half a length. The farthest screen reported on the historic Dominican baseball rivalry between the Licey Tigres and the Águilas of Cibao.

At about 9:15 the door to the bar opened again, and someone came in, studied the room, and finally headed for the corner by the slot machine. He told some secret to the solitary man in black, and the scarce light revealed an angry scowl. Again the one in black rubbed his leg underneath the pants, as if assuring himself that all remained in readiness.

Hanging as I'd been on the old man's story and the tense game on TV (La Russa now kicked the dirt to protest a call on a close play at second base), I had almost forgotten the lone man. He looked toward our side of the room while saying something to his visitor. Maybe it was "Wait for me outside." I needed to hide my interest, as the detectives of my weekly shows advise in the case of a whiff of danger. But again I wondered why I always had to act as if I were Columbo. Very simple, a resigned voice inside me answered: Those of us who bet can't lose ourselves in the game, because we need to calculate the final result.

I managed to direct my eyes back to the middle screen, but I couldn't order my ears to ignore the old man's words, which were getting more and more interesting. I owe the monologue that came next (a monologue because the younger man only nodded as the older one talked) to a Yadier Molina triple. That hit by the St. Louis catcher scored Matt Holliday from first, tying the game at two runs apiece, and that's how it stayed until the ninth inning. My hopes were falling fast. God did not appear to be taking signs from me.

The old man, on the other hand, seemed cheered by this new turn of the game. He looked over the paper on which he'd written down his bets and went on with his story, to which I was all ears.

"When I was young, I managed the amateur team in our town in the south. One of the star prospects was my son. A big, strong boy who had the scouts talking about a new Rico Carty. The comparison to Rico really didn't do justice to my boy, because power wasn't his only tool. He was a terrific fielder and on top of that he had speed. He was no truck, he was a gazelle. There wasn't any doubt he'd be better than the slugger from San Pedro de Macorís—with all due respect to Carty, you know? And he had brains, smart like the Alous, like Juan Marichal. I could imagine him managing in the big leagues when he got old.

"The scouts kept after me, wearing me out, and the press was after me, too. The day of his signing approached, and we'd prepared everything for the family celebration we were going to have. . . . Then, the hurricane came."

After this sentence, he seemed to clear a lump from his throat. In the mirror I could see that the memory was getting him down, and the effects of the whiskey were hitting him, too. His face relived the time he was talking about. He signaled to the blonde, who came over, reached into her blouse, and handed him the paper that had been warming against her breast. The old man whispered something to her while glancing at the solitary man out of the corner of his eye. She nodded, yes.

"Are you sure?" the man with the battered briefcase asked. "The same team?"

"Yes, definitely. St. Louis," she answered. She turned away to attend to other customers.

His eye on the man in black in the darkened corner, the old man raised his glass in a toast. "To the Cardinals!" he announced dramatically, "though I've never thought much of that team. To St. Louis, because today I want to forget what that fucking hurricane did, twisting fate and drowning the future of a great prospect!"

Clearly the hurricane he was talking about was Georges, that freak of nature with torrential rains and winds over one hundred twenty miles an hour that scourged the island in 1998, provoking death and desolation through most of the country and the Republic of Haiti next door.

"The river rose," the old man continued, and now he too rose, coming to his feet, turning away from the screen but still following the game through the mirrors. Ninth inning, tied, Cardinals at bat with two outs and men on first and third. La Russa, in a duel of strategies, called on Pujols to pinch-hit. "That river ruined our life, my family's and mine. It took my son. He was found two days later up in a tree. With one leg smashed and his face frozen in fear."

Atlanta made a pitching change. I took advantage of the break to go to the john. When I got back, the old man had fallen into a deep silence. The young one in the checkered shirt was no longer nodding but was trying to cheer him up. At the same time, the lone man in black with the nervous tic had stood up again. As I passed him I realized how big he was, enormous. He wouldn't need a pistol if he wanted to kill someone. I remembered Inspector Morse and deduced that the old man's briefcase could be a ruse to distract visitors from the real danger. My deduction took on force when, unexpectedly, the lone man staggered toward the slot machine. "He's pretending to be drunk," I thought. "He's got an accomplice waiting outside, and now he's playing drunk." Using the mirrors, I kept my eye on the other two. "Nobody's catching me off guard," I swore.

The old man sat down and sighed deeply. In silence his eyes went from screen to screen as mine had done before. Armstrong took off, closely pursued by Alberto Contador. Surprisingly, Roddick lost the second set to a revived Federer, conscious of playing for history. Holyfield bounced like an angry cat because Tyson had bitten him on the ear. There was no more horse race, but a documentary about the death of the King of Pop. On the last screen Polonia (always him!) crashed into the wall in a Tigres vs. Águilas game.

Glass in hand, the old man shifted his eyes back to the center screen and began to offer his analysis of the game. The lone man in black in the corner watched him with a condemnatory look half shrouded in shadow. Surely these two were in cahoots. Again I felt I ought to get out of there. What was really in the briefcase? I hadn't learned much from either my analyses modeled on Kojak and Columbo or the psychological insights of Inspector Morse.

I prepared for the worst. There was someone waiting outside. I was going to be attacked on the street, not inside the bar. But not till after the game.

Top of the ninth. Men at the corners, two outs, Boone Logan on the mound facing the pinch-hitting Pujols at the plate, play resumed. Curve ball. Grounder to third, picked up by Chipper Jones, throw to first. End of half inning, game still tied.

I breathed again. La Russa's strategy had failed, and things soon got worse for St. Louis. In the bottom of the ninth, Atlanta put a man on second after two outs. Garrett Anderson at bat, breaking ball, slow roller to first—and through Pujols's legs! Victory to the Atlanta Braves.

My team had lost, but I was happy because Atlanta's win brought me several thousand pesos.

In the bathroom, where no one could see, I slid an empty bottle into my pocket, just in case. I was getting ready to collect on my bet and leave when the old man suddenly picked up the piece of cardboard from the floor, grabbed the briefcase, and stood. I thought he was after me, but no. He sat back down, then signaled to the solitary man. I thought of sprinting out the door and leaving my winnings behind, but the two girls were watching me and I felt ashamed. Better for those guys to kill me than for the women to think I was a coward. I was moving toward the cash register when the old man opened the case and said to the younger one in the checkered shirt, "Look, here are all the clippings. Here's the whole story, so all the snoopers, all the busybodies can see I'm not lying." He sought out my face with a cynical look. "You, don't you see now?"

They were a mix of sports articles and news pieces covering the havoc wreaked by Hurricane Georges long ago. There were a lot of stories about the home run battle between Sammy Sosa and Mark McGwire in that same September of 1998. There was a half-page photo below a headline that proclaimed, "Emeterio Ramírez Cadet, top prospect." On the cardboard, alongside that article that also showed a small, poor house and the parents and siblings of the young player posing for the camera, the old man had glued a feature that said, "Fate Catches Up With the Future Pro." The old man read solemnly (no more music to compete with his voice) how the Nizao River had buried houses, people, and animals after the hurricane came through.

Tears fell from his bitter eyes. Shaking, he threw the paper the blonde had given him to the floor while he cursed the local authorities who had left him defenseless. The lone man from the darkened table approached with difficulty. He had waited until almost all the customers were gone, I saw. The girls inched off to the side as if in fear. He said to the old man, "Let's go. The taxi's been waiting for a while. Did I hear that you bet on St. Louis? Me too. Bad luck."

Then they left, each supporting the other as they walked. The door closed, erasing them.

I signaled to the blonde, who was gathering empty glasses and bottles. "Who's that guy staggering from his *jumo*?" I used the local term to make myself clear.

"He's not drunk, he doesn't touch a drop. I'm surprised you don't know about him. They call him The Prospect, his name is Emeterio. He comes every night to look after Don Enemencio, his father, who owns this place. Emeterio lost his leg during Georges, and his father feels guilty about it."

I leaned down to pick up the note the old man had dropped. I opened it and read, "Let's go, papa. I can't get used to this metal leg."

THE STRANGE GAME OF THE MEN IN BLUE

José Bobadilla
(Dominican Republic)

José Bobadilla (Santo Domingo, 1955) traces his formation as a writer to mentors ranging from Aurora Tavárez Belliard, who taught him to read, to Juan Bosch, his most important influence. He spent 1980 to 1986 in Nicaragua, first as a literacy volunteer, then as a professor. After his return home, he served as an assistant to Bosch and a member of the Presidential Council on Culture. He was awarded the national literary prize for the novel Memoria del horror hermoso in 2007 and the following year for the story collection La insaciable aguja del deseo. He is currently a special assistant to the president of the Dominican Republic.

Though set in an unnamed country in the nineteenth century, this story borrows the surname of the military governor of the Dominican Republic during the US occupation of 1916–24, Rear Admiral Harry Shepard Knapp.

For weeks the city had known that this would not be any ordinary day. Admiral Knapp, scrupulous in all things from brushing his teeth to the extraordinary challenge of a difficult battle, wrote in his diary in his customary cramped script:

The festivities will take place on the fourth of the coming month. The players will make their entrance right behind the marine band that will follow the flagbearers with marches and patriotic songs. In the meantime, three nights earlier, we shall carry out the sentence that puts an end, once and for all, to the bandits who so embarrassed us in the recent skirmishes.

So wrote that officer, a man who instructed his bootblack to work as if polishing the most fragile of mirrors while, to himself, he silently intoned old songs of the South, that ever-more-elusive ancestral paradise where solicitous black women served him breakfast while his lover of the previous night stirred in voluptuous slumber between the sheets. Spencer Walker O'Sullivan Knapp—of the O'Sullivans of Memphis, Clayton River, and St. Louis—was forty-nine years old, appropriately tall if a bit ungainly, with a somber, penetrating voice and gestures more deliberate than spontaneous. His blond hair had a reddish tint that made it look dyed, while the twinkle in his eyes called to mind the flashing silhouette of a tiny fishhook in a cup of some disturbing azure brew. There were some who enthusiastically averred that he was a veteran of European wars, those clashes of kings and generals on horseback, stranded here to expiate a secret guilt. Indeed, in furtive written notes or over elegant strokes of the billiard cue, it was said that none less than the president of his native land had summoned him and declared, in a fit of uncharacteristic frankness, "You'll be an admiral at last, but you'll have no fleet to command."

Thus was he condemned to dress in full formal regalia in a place located, so to speak, on the outskirts of a courtyard where beggars from the poorest neighborhoods gathered to pick over the leavings of disdainful gentlemen attending the ball. But the admiral gave little or no thought to such matters. The Fourth arrived with a jumble of flags, pennants, and bunting hung like sacred altar cloths from every available perch. At dawn, a bugle call summoned the troops to formation, and a cannon shot thundered from the ramparts for all to set their clocks and pocket watches by, so that at nine sharp, without a second's delay, the celebration could begin. The first to arrive were the honorable judges of the Supreme Court in their long ritual robes. Then, just as the chords of the country's most august patriotic hymn reached a crescendo, the Most Reverend Monsignor made his appearance out of the shade of a long line of ancient trees, like a spectral apparition wrapped in frozen flames of taffeta, solemn under a three-peaked biretta, and took his seat upon his ceremonial throne.

The ill feeling that festered between the two principal figures now appeared irresolvable, since neither flattery nor threats had served the haughty officer to lessen the archbishop's longstanding sense of injury. Indeed, His Reverence made a point of attending every public ceremony and state function, never missing a chance to display his disdain. It must be admitted that Spencer Knapp's punctilious courtesy had become proverbial. Yet, surrounded by his no-less-correct general staff, he observed the natives of the country as if from a distant street or, worse still, a balcony high above.

A junior officer on horseback approached the reviewing stand at a ceremonial trot. Coming to an abrupt halt, he uttered something that did not require any translation. The admiral responded with a gesture that was in turn answered with an energetic salute. At this signal, as if activated by a perfect train of gears, gun batteries fired to signal the corps of marines to parade in formation before the multitude. However, this was not what anyone had come to see. Behind the marines, a double file of athletes descended from the gun batteries like the spreading tail of a peacock, the column on the right in shirts of a celestial blue, and that on the left in scarlet. Upon the parade ground, a mysterious square shape had been drawn with limestone dust. The protagonists immediately occupied this playing field, each in his designated place. The strange sport they were about to demonstrate was said to be an invention of prehistoric Indians bored to distraction during the long winters, and later perfected with martial discipline and artistic flourishes by fortune-hunters and ruffians. Following long-standing rules and regulations that made some sense out of nonsense, these sportsmen banged away at a small ball while dashing like lunatics between pillows spread about the field. The cognoscenti of this pursuit referred to the square space as a diamond and the objective of their activity as a run.

Was that all? Nothing but the whacking of an insignificant little leather ball? Could there be a diversion for the masses that lacked the atavistic dignity of spilled blood, the grandeur of a willing sacrifice, the risk of death or even sometimes death itself? Wasn't such a courtesy required to dress up the onerous task of teaching proper behavior? Not even Christ himself, in his right mind, would have thought of disappointing the masses by denying them the supreme offering of his crucifixion. All this being true, the content of the game about to unfold could not be what was stirring the crowd. Rather, some word must have leaked out about the participation of three black men, with the stature of giants, who were now suddenly spotted by a woman in the audience, as evidenced by her heaving breast and vociferous cries. Their attention thus attracted, others spread the news. The local men recently trained to join the contest on the foreigners' payroll bore the everyday names of Juanico Cañongo, Indalecio Bendito, and Ñungo Calderón. They paraded onto the field like unexpected cards tumbling from a gambler's sleeve, causing the monsignor to rub his eyes, because the trick being played by the foreign authorities had to be seen to be believed. And at first sight it smacked of barefaced betrayal. It was one thing for his flock to assemble to watch the gringos brandish sticks and bang at balls, but quite another to participate in this spectacle that insulted rather than amused. Yet there they stood, like recently washed fighting bulls, ensconced among the invaders who waited for their admiral in his fringed uniform and feathered cap to honor the impending entertainment by tossing out the first of the spheres.

The participation of three of their own brought out a growing multitude that soon packed the fortress. It did not matter very much that the native-born players were mere supplementary patches sewn quickly into the folds of the red-shirted team. Although the game was being played primarily by Yankees, the unexpected local participants gave the spectacle new meaning. Knapp smiled. He shot his honored guests an insolent look, for he was sure he had made the right decision. At least on this occasion he had managed to arrange things to impart a genuine glow to what he wished to honor. He saw that the crowd had, of its own volition, brought forward La Niña Mejía, conveying her to the front row and seating her on the wall. Still very attractive, she was the city's highest-ranking lady of the night, well known to be the lover-in-case-of-emergency of the most important gentlemen. It would be foolish for those on the reviewing stand to pretend not to recognize her. Neither the admiral nor the monsignor nor Don Ubaldo Rondón de la Cierva, the chief justice who performed the duties of president of the Republic, tried to hide his shock at seeing the bruises and black eyes upon La Mejía's normally immaculate face. Never before had she shown signs of such an attack, yet today she exhibited them with provocative nerve. It was true, of course, that long immersion in a combustible mixture of dalliance and flirtation could bring consequences, and on more than one occasion the city had mourned the death of a maenad of bodily pleasure. But who would dare to take such liberties with La Mejía, who accepted caresses and coins only from the most select? For a moment she seemed to shoot a glance of pain, spite, and accusation toward the seats of honor, but she was following the lead of the entire crowd, which was directing its intention to Knapp as he approached the field to hurl the minuscule ball, now wrapped in a garish silk ribbon, toward the corner where a player awaited it with one of the sticks or clubs, also beribboned, as the signal for the contest to begin.

Immediately after, one thrower took up his position in the center of the field while a powerful club handler in the designated corner awaited the delivery. Would such a ridiculously small item as the tiny leather sphere be able to awaken the sleeping emotions of the multitude? Equally lacking in elegance were the sticks—officially denominated "bats"—and the flat, cakelike objects the players wore on their hands, the shabbiest excuses for gloves, to be used to interrupt the projectile's solitary flight. Suddenly bat met ball with a downward chop that sent the sphere rolling through the grass, surely nothing of importance, but the batter ran like a madman toward one of the pillows marking the boundary. He remained there while another stick-wielder took his place in the spot where it had all begun. The thrower gave him a searching look, as if weighing some secret knowledge, as if the ball could fly with the living intelligence of a mysterious bird, a wingless moon that never allowed itself to be trapped. The blue team was batting against the red, as befitted the opening frame of a special game to mark the solemn commemoration.

The batter, a rather sullen young man, somehow read the fleeting thoughts of the rapidly advancing ball. With a swing that was beautiful in its rhythm, he made contact and drove it to the leftmost boundary of the field, where the parade ground ended at the cliffs overlooking the sea. The runner on the first of the bases, electrified by the majestic flight of the ball, sprinted to the third one, while the hitter who had unleashed the shot reached the spot the first man had left. The game had taken a favorable turn for the blue team, an augury fulfilled when the next batter hit a line drive to the center of the field, allowing the two men on base to score easily. The pair of runs was duly recorded with chalk on a large scoreboard by the diminutive scribe who served in one of the offices, now puffed with pride that seemed to make him larger than life. For players who considered themselves skilled at the game and the equal of their opponents, surrendering two runs in the first inning was a hard pill to swallow. The audience, however, having come to the game in complete ignorance of the rules, attracted only by the presence of their three countrymen who had been secretly trained to take part in this important event, neither applauded nor stirred. Rather, they found themselves in the position of anyone who attends a weighty speech or sermon delivered in a foreign language and must rely on inferences from tone of voice, or moments of stridency and heat, at best deciphering a sudden gesture here or there.

At this moment, a soldier approached Admiral Knapp to whisper a message in his ear, suddenly bringing a new expression to his face. With enforced calm in keeping with his rigid manners, the officer stared vacantly at the crowd. He stroked the golden belt buckle of his dress uniform and, begging the pardon of those around him, he left. His aides likewise disappeared into the tower of the fortress, reappearing en masse on the outer side of the upper battlements. Surely the admiral's departure from the game was a mistake that, even if involuntary, diminished him before the other dignitaries. What grave occurrence could have caused it? Many eyes were upon him, as always happens to those in high positions who must live and die within narrow cages of glass. Thus, everyone saw Knapp point the long, thin finger of a telescope toward the northern plains, to investigate more closely something that must have raised a deep shadow of fear and rage in his mind. Luckily for him, a burst of applause among scattered exclamations served as diversion, a puff of smoke emerging opportunely from a magician's handkerchief and wand. The admiral now disappeared from the ramparts and soon resumed his place of honor before the sharp gaze of Counselor Rondón, the first magistrate of the Republic, and his bitter enemy, the Reverend Monsignor.

"Something unexpected, your Excellency?"

It was impossible for those two men, who for some trifling reason never spoke in front of third parties, to be completely ignorant of what was afoot. All reports indicated that on this very day of celebration, the self-proclaimed general Aquiles Contreras intended to enter the capital. According those same reports, however, there was little or nothing to worry about in terms of defense. To cancel the sporting event that the occupation troops had organized would only offer gratuitous comfort and substance to the enemy—especially since Spencer Knapp was confident that nothing in the innermost life or soul of the guerrilla general could escape being recorded between the covers of a leather portfolio polished to such perfection as to match the glow of his knee-high boots, a portfolio that rested on the shining surface of his desk and contained what were referred to as Special Reports. The monsignor, for his part, was a haughty and capricious prelate, cut to the mold of an office that for thousands of years had commanded respect by inspiring fear. Although this made him rather predictable, he managed to fortify himself behind a reputation for unchallenged integrity. If others believe—or are disposed to believe—that one is good, then one is indeed good unless and until something happens to shake one's position. Justice Ubaldo Rondón was a different matter. His perpetual smile was like a bloody knife on a velvet napkin, a rigid steel weapon that hung from his flowing, fierce mustache, its gleam gaining color and depth when his eyes so desired. He was skilled at conveying the impression he could see everything without even looking.

Given all this, as well as the lethargic pace at which things unfolded, could there be any truth to reports predicting the entrance of a defiant and perhaps even victorious Contreras into the heart of the capital?

In Knapp's case, he simply could not let go of his first impression of the enemy who—in the shaky handwriting of a reluctant schoolboy—was reported to be the illegitimate son of a certain Sinforoso Rodríguez, a rich farmer in the south who, attempting to shake off the demons so easily invoked by the boy's sharp-witted mother, sent him to be brought up among the robes and skirts of priests and nuns and then (in accord with the custom of his cockfight companions) dispatched him for polishing to no less a place than Paris, from which he returned with French tastes and the title of physician, a profession he deemed inappropriate for his temperament and therefore never practiced. There were, of course, other versions. One of these, without contradicting the first one, cast him as the haphazard descendant of a black emperor in Africa. Another, credited by many, held him to be nothing less than the milk nephew of Don Ubaldo, which in popular parlance meant someone brought up alongside the offspring of the magistrate, perhaps the child of their wet-nurse indeed. Other claims, as foolish as they were widespread, attributed his messianic proclivities to quite different bloodlines, whether that of a particular secular demon or of Christopher Columbus himself. Why, we might ask, is it so hard to explain any man's actions without recourse to the mania of making him the son of someone, and thus explaining both his ambitions and his circumstances by means of a pedestrian, one-dimensional vision that attributes any and all destinies to lineage and family? All agreed that Contreras had to descend from some august household and that fate, itself corralled into a very narrow channel, had decreed that the rebel and the gringo should share the same woman. Yes, the Niña Mejía, who (being very young when all this began) could not have imagined, even given the most portentous of omens, that the middling handsome youth who embraced her so ardently night after night would find himself in a fight to the death with the Yankee commander—now, years later, with the country in the throes of a domestic war that had opened the way to a dishonorable invasion.

But, in all honesty, what did it matter? Whether lord or beggar, Contreras was there, in command of an invisible army that would follow him into the teeth of sworn annihilation, and what was worse, for Knapp's purposes, was that he had proved impossible to capture. Everyone offered the admiral smiles, but their respect and their money went to Contreras in proportion to his deeds. If his hazardous insurrection had suffered its ups and downs, still the effects of his sustained attacks had made themselves felt in outbreaks of resistance under the noses of the marines and in the remotest corners of the nation. These included fearful assaults such as the battle at Barranca de los García, from which Knapp's troops had to withdraw bearing their dead and wounded in shame. Worse still, Spencer Knapp could not learn to let go of his first impression. Carried away by the apparent clarity of his provincial outlook, he wrote in the meticulous tidiness of his diary, in some despair:

The people of this land have arms and legs, that is to say, torso, head, and extremities. But neither the infinite shades of their skins nor the elemental simplicities of their minds reach the stature required to define them as men in the full sense of the word. Our case is different. We are human. They are not.

And so he let his emotions convince him that differences in external decoration confirmed his superiority (though these were nothing more than a skin-tight biological disguise). He let that belief be buttressed by the most logical of sophistries and let it extend from himself to what was external: to the size and strength of the army he commanded and the wondrous mechanisms that had created it. Therefore, he and his forces were fated to govern a world of debased remnants of humanity that could have no other destiny but to submit. His pride found itself reduced to this frighteningly childish belief and its associated rites and customs, made most visible in the majestic carved and painted eagles adorning the fortress's barracks and storehouses and his resplendent personal office most of all. To Knapp it was unthinkable that a nobody like Contreras could defeat him. Further—and this was worse—it was unthinkable that others of the rebel's ilk could be right about anything at all. Of course, such a presumption had to be hidden from the public, who must not sniff even the faintest whiff of the contents of the books and journals Knapp so avidly read in private. Perhaps those opinions could be expressed, occasionally, within the confines of a lewd joke that served as escape valve for the repugnance produced by everything around him. Such ideas were the fruit of a long, silent, unexamined gestation that nourished the darkest parts of his heart. They were a clumsy and irrelevant justification, which a closer look at his surroundings would have toppled to the ground. Haven't we been told, since the dawn of historical time, how Cain judged Abel and then destroyed him? In this way, Spencer Knapp was no more foolish than the soldiers who served him as advisors, nor was he a lesser man than the antediluvian chaplain who soothed any doubts about his duties with all manner of rationales. Whenever we give power to another, we know what he may be capable of in the depths of his soul.

Upset as he was by news of Contreras's advance, Knapp did not take in the extent of the public ovation greeting the three mulatto players. The first of them to hit was Indalecio Bendito, a well-built young man with a gladiator's bearing. The bat seemed a child's plaything in this youth's strong hands, as he patiently let the first two pitches go by. All indications suggested that both teams already knew him well. The *pitcher* was noticeably tense, and so was the player crouching to receive the ball nearly in the pathway of the bat. Buoyed by the crowd, Indalecio Bendito took careful measure of his adversaries and succeeded in giving the ball such an unexpected blow that it disappeared into the sea. The seaside cliff stood just to the south of the fortress, its height obviating the need for any wall or other system of protection. But the nearby lower cannon emplacement, beside which the wall for victims of the firing squad had been built, made the waters below an equally fatal location for any craft daring to approach the dock. Bendito, proudly and with great care as if handling a slim sliver of glass, lay his bat on the ground and, amidst wild cheering from the crowd, proceeded at a walking pace around the square, duly scoring the run that his towering four-base hit had earned. No one observing his muscles could doubt that such a feat was within his power. Even the sergeant serving as umpire, unaware of the involuntary lapse, greeted the hitter effusively as he crossed the plate. When Indalecio reached the long bench where the other players were waiting, however, the team captain confronted him angrily. "Why didn't you run? Why didn't you circle the bases at the speed our rules require?"

Indalecio Bendito, who was never at a loss for words, hesitated. Whether or not he liked what he had done, he knew that the words of Corporal Jack Perry contained a dangerous truth. But his mockery, if that's what it was, had already been committed. As if to calm the waters, the next batter—Lance-Corporal Bruce Palmer, a Viking cyclops equal in size to Bendito—advanced to the plate, where he repeated the black man's feat, adding another run. That was what the game was all about.

Interrupted by the events on the field, Admiral Knapp had left Counselor Rondón's casual question unanswered. Avoiding the magistrate's bleary eyes, the admiral clapped him on the shoulder in a comradely way as if that constituted an answer. Then Knapp left again, this time for the solitude of his office. As he reached for his pipe to refill it with tobacco, La Niña Mejía took him unawares. A few tears betrayed tumultuous waters deep inside. The admiral was disturbed. One could not trust a whore, of course, but she had come to confront him with her best weapons. Confident of her powers, she approached him and spoke with fearful gravity.

"Sir, this is going to be a terrible day."

Spencer Knapp could clearly see the scratches and bruises that had surprised all observers. They seemed so out of place on a woman known for her composure. In spite of her office, she never made scenes, much less appeared in public bearing the marks of anyone's rage, a condition both sad and beneath her dignity. The admiral, who for some curious reason always thought of an eight-ball when he saw her, rested his hands on a silver paperweight. Flattered by the weakness she was displaying, he blurted out, "Do you love me?"

That was going too far. The naïveté of such a question, even if asked without thinking, pierced her like an ornamental pin that is suddenly stained with blood. It was she who had provoked this encounter, of course; she had shed a few tears for him; she was here now with something intangible in hand, repayment of debt owing to some degree of tenderness. But love him? Having grown strong, or perhaps impervious, in the tiresome labor of offering pleasure, she could not accept the defeat of succumbing to love. Letting her shock show, she stepped away. With the grossest of chuckles, deceiving him as she did herself, she demanded, "Is your intent to force me to lie?"

Still, in some way this answer was a false card laid on the table. And also her worst card, her least intelligent move. Though aware of her difficult role, she did in fact want to play. She was doing so, without knowing exactly why, by betting on a rebellious sense of loyalty that betrayed her. Though Aquiles Contreras apparently no longer had any feeling for her, he represented a collective past, an entire way of being of which she was a part. Like it or not, this universe of imperatives and eventualities perforce included her.

"My premonition will have to be enough for you," she

added. "I can't step beyond the bounds of that darkened room."

And now it was as if she were already seeing him dead, laid out in an expensive coffin, shining in the cold light of four wax tapers. There he lay in his dress uniform of luxurious trappings from the dazzlingly polished boots to the gold braid at his collar, from which his head emerged like a withered flower shut up in the definitive peace of his private and irrevocable death. She turned her back. She knew, as a woman, that she was leaving behind an inconstant man. She was relieved to be rid of the uncomfortable baggage. She was ready to live like someone who drives off in a carriage among new friends, a carriage that advances, unconcerned, while no one looks back.

After she was gone, Spencer Knapp emerged from his office and returned to the reviewing stand. With his face bathed by an emotion he couldn't feel, he searched stolidly for La Niña Mejía among the crowd, but all he saw was how much the multitude had grown—and more, how it had changed, how some transformation was at work in each of its members, how this same woman who would offer her body for a few coins and receive his most intimate spasms could now, strangely, rise triumphant in the illustrious figure of His Reverence the Monsignor and equally in the threat posed by the mild-mannered Justice Ubaldo Rincón. She was even embodied in the troubling presence of his own officers, star witnesses mutely signing an absurdly blank page.

The ball game, of course, was still going on. It moved along, sometimes quickly and sometimes slowly, as decreed by the straitjacket of a rhythm that, nonetheless, refused to reveal what the end would be. The crowd, now packed threateningly into every inch of the parade ground, came to life only when the mulattos Calderón, Bendito, and Cañongo stepped up to bat. Which they did, now, with notably different results. Calderón, besides the strength common to all three, possessed an elegance like that of a palm tree waving in the breeze, a greeting that awoke the utmost jealousy in the rest of the men, while most of the women accepted it without the slightest blush. But Calderón made no effort, barely exerting himself enough to strike out before returning intact to the bench. There he listened to the frenzied cries with which the public greeted the lightning shots of his compatriots, both of them *hits* that advanced their teammates around the bases. As the sun reached its height, the contest came to an end without a winner, though not before Bendito took advantage of a mistake by the hurler to hit a second *cuadrangular*, as did a sergeant named Conrad Burns, a cook's assistant most of the time but today enjoying the opposite face of power. With the score tied, a technical decision was reached to leave it that way, because the game had to end at the appointed hour. The military band reemerged behind the fluttering colors, followed by a ceremonial wheeled cannon that fired a protocol shot, the command to spread the copious meal that would blanket the offensive stench of the moral corpse rotting underneath. What place was there for happiness except within such a lie, playing along, exchanging scornful, oft-repeated jokes, the sorts of tragic jokes that never make anyone laugh?

Knapp and his guests ate and drank at the table of honor, as planned, under the welcome shade of a roof that had been raised by a previous power. What remained of that power now? Only the mute, indifferent stones, heaped one upon another like an argument constructed out of the phrases closest to hand, yet retaining the form and content of a fallacy from long ago. When weariness laid waste to what was left of the day, Spencer Knapp had the rash idea he should go to La Niña Mejía, should present himself to be loved. Unconsciously, what he wanted was to dissipate his anger, give the lie to her foreboding, take revenge by possessing her. Revenge on whom? On himself, perhaps, as well as all the rest. La Niña Mejia merely fulfilled her office. At first she made him wait, sending a message that she was indisposed, letting him cool his heels among younger women and tinkling songs. But that was an empty gesture, an errant one that led her nowhere, so finally her embroidered card invited him to enter. He found her naked and smiling, like a different woman. She kissed him exuberantly, yet as mechanically as a bell responding to the pull of a string.

"Give it to me," she said. "Give me whatever is left of you."

The unaccustomed frankness, the coarse familiarity appealed to Spencer. La Niña Mejía had never been like this, but if she could be, all the better. It was like opening the shutters alongside an unknown garden and enjoying the splendid fragrance that rushed into the silent dark, even while thick window bars kept the garden firmly out of reach. Her body's surrender was that way too, her charms as undeniable as they were fleeting, as if her nakedness were clothed in the somber attire of one lone occasion of intimate use, one lone exception to the rule. After the brief encounter, his delight faded. He found himself set aside like a heavy tome closed after reading and placed on the table nearest to hand. As for her, when all was said and done, she had been used as on so many other occasions to provide relief and nothing more. Reckoning up her need to be alone, she wrapped herself in a robe and left the room. Returning with a cup of tea, she knew that something important was lacking in this man, that in truth she felt neither pity for him nor any desire except to see him leave. Though she was not expecting any other visitors tonight, she wanted him gone. But not through the door by which he had entered, so once he was dressed she opened another one that led to a different way out. In this passage Knapp heard words and laughter that, through no one's fault, led him to a luxurious sofa holding Counselor Rondón. The magistrate could not see the admiral, nor was he in condition to do so. The woman cleared her throat.

"I don't need to add anything to what you already know," she pointed out logically. "Don Ubaldo has always been a visitor to our honorable home."

That was true, of course. The intelligence reports that so often burdened Knapp with new and pressing truths, carelessly woven among inconsistent details, had given him entry to an endless labyrinth of personal information, whether openly presented or left to be inferred. Since he counted this knowledge among his instruments of power, there was no point or credibility in feigning surprise. With one foot out the door, he had to ask the only question that really mattered to him, the one that had brought him here whether he knew it or not.

"Why did you warn me of a terrible day?"

The woman met his gaze with rigid, angry candor, suspended like a wildflower over the wound of an almost perfect smile.

"I don't know. We've always been at war. This time, it's against you."

Someone was coming down the street, so it was time for him to leave. His two bodyguards appeared to escort him, one on either side.

"We didn't want to interrupt you, but there's something you need to know before you reach the fort. The three Negros who played on our teams were brutally murdered."

Was this a bad joke? Who thought they had the right to challenge his authority that way? Murdered? Was that really what one of the two soldiers flanking him had said? The other, as if rectifying a grave error, added a hair-raising detail to complete his companion's report.

"It happened just now," he said. "That is, right when they returned to their homes. Everything indicates the killers were waiting for them. Their heads are on a bench in the barracks."

They passed through the streets of the small city, deserted because of the gruesome news, as if all were shielding themselves from an earthquake whose rage would reach them no matter what. At the entrance to the stronghold, Knapp noticed for the first time what was written there—*His Majesty Carlos III*—and more besides, short phrases that informed anyone entering the gate or merely passing by, like incantations from a much thumbed grimoire. The severed heads of Cañongo, Calderón, and Bendito were unmistakable, debris left behind by the error of recruiting them to play. A shiver deep inside testified to his elemental terror, the extreme condensation of all the hatreds he harbored. Without further ado, he shut himself in his room. Too many things had happened today, a day that the delicate hands of his lovely French clock said was coming to a close. Perhaps what was left of the night would grant him a reprieve. Unable to sleep, he automatically lit a lamp. A childish impulse drove him to the large mirror in whose depths his image appeared like a huge, looming ghost. Could that really be he? Was that truly Spencer Knapp, beholding his other self like a small child being told the story of what he will become, who he will be in the end? With the bitter intuition that this moment could swell into a chapter that would consume the rest of any man's life, he filled his pipe and headed for the tower—for the cool, refreshing immensity of the open sky, clear as it so often was and blanketed with stars. Out in the air, he felt he had reached the home of an old friend who would hear him without complaint. He was an admiral. There was no doubt of this, he was the admiral, the absolute lord of the dark majesty of this deep hour of the night. The soldiers on watch snapped to attention when they recognized his long silk robe. In a corner of the courtyard, in one of the great open trunks where all the furled flags and banners had been laid, rested the bats, balls, and gloves. All they were good for now was provoking a memory, and upon that memory floated the burdensome ghosts of the three ill-starred blacks.

The vast tranquility of the moment rendered all precautions moot. There was only a ticking remnant that promised his soul peace and a tangible result. Knapp climbed toward the battlements. The city lay prostrate beneath him, intact and silent like the buried spine of a forgotten monster. Breathing deeply so as to fill his soul with the power of things, he leaned out over the embrasure, on the side of the tower that faced the river and, beyond, the slow swells of the sea. In the lookout's box, like a murmur escaping from the ashes of one long dead, stood an inoffensive figure in a frock coat and glowing spectacles that must have been framed in gold. The figure uttered a single short sentence, fondling every syllable while pointing the mouth of a gun at the officer's forehead.

"Admiral Spencer Walker O'Sullivan Knapp, here I am."

CLOCK REACHES THE EMPEROR'S CITADEL

Rafael Acevedo
(Puerto Rico)

Rafael Acevedo (Santurce, 1960) is a poet, novelist, and editor. He has been the editor of the magazine Filo de Juego, of the cultural supplement to the weekly Claridad, and of the publishing house La Secta de Los Perros. His novel Exquisito cadáver won a Casa de las Américas (Cuba) prize in 2001. Poems from his six books of poetry (most recently Eligía franca, 2015) have appeared in several anthologies of Latin American and Puerto Rican poetry and in English translation in Guernica Magazine, Two Lines, and Words Without Borders.

As in the "The Strange Game of the Men in Blue," in Acevedo's novel Flor de Ciruelo y el viento (Plum Blossom and the Wind) the diamond game appears as seen by eyes that have never seen it before. This time we are in a more playful work, set in a mock-medieval China where a character called Zhong, or Clock, the mechanic in charge of all the water clocks in the Emperor's main palace, flees his job to search for his missing brother and becomes legendary as "the peaceful warrior," both for his battles with bandits and swindlers and for his avoidance of battle when possible. Finally, he agrees to accompany ten of the Emperor's soldiers to go see the ruler, whom he has never met in person.

After ten days riding at a comfortable pace, the ten soldiers and the peaceful warrior reached the citadel where the Emperor was residing incognito. It was a structure of only a hundred rooms in which the supreme ruler liked to escape from the cares of administering the navel of the world. In a low-lying area, Clock saw a group of men, divided into two opposing bands, carrying out a strange rite.

At the sound of a gong, nine men clad in striking indigo robes and orange hats ran full tilt onto a terrain demarcated by straight lines traced out in pure white lime. On the left side, a chorus of Buddhist monks chanted lively mantras as if tossing them into the air. On the opposite side, soldiers responded with trumpet blasts and the plucking of lutes. Multicolored pennants adorned the festival. Clock noticed that the men in indigo, now standing relatively still in positions mimicking those of the stars in the night sky, wore grotesque gloves that seemed to be made of yak skin, but only on one hand. Though no expert on the Zodiac, he thought the figures were grouped to look rather like the Great Bear.

One of the nine gentlemen in indigo stood on top of a small hill and from there he threw a sphere that seemed to be made of white marble to a crouching confederate with the trappings of a samurai. Then Clock saw an adversary approach the man receiving the sphere. The adversary was decked out in similar colors but inverted—with a bright orange robe and an indigo cap. Turning to regard the warrior on the hill, he brandished a stylized club in his hands. He touched the club to a pentagon lying on the ground and then took up a position of attack.

If this rite was a simulation of combat, Clock thought, the warrior in the crouch needed only to knock down the one brandishing the club, or the one with the club should surrender in view of the numerical advantage of the gentlemen in indigo. However, this did not seem to be the point of the ceremony. An old man attired in deep black raised his hands and shouted *Kía*. All went silent, and the warrior on the hill launched the sphere with all his might. The man with the club feinted at it, then let it go by. *Da!* said the sage dressed in black, as the samurai contained the sphere in his large glove of yak skin. With a satisfied expression, the samurai returned the sphere to the warrior on the hill. The monks on the left side let sounds of complaint escape their mouths. A crane crossed the sky, letting out a hoarse croaking sound, an omen, perhaps. The warrior on the hill raised his leg and, in a graceful motion, threw the object again. This time the man smashed into the marble sphere with his club. Soldiers, monks, and all began to emit howls. The man with the club ran to a square marker some twenty paces from the pentagon. Ignorant as he was of the whole animated ceremony, Clock could not fathom the chaos that this unleashed. When he was about to inquire the meaning of such a pageant or simulation, he was interrupted.

"Here we are."

• • •

The palatial structure seemed to have been built to blend in with the land—as if an enormous rock had been hollowed out into halls, chambers, passages, and stairways. The external walls were covered in ivy, whose berries sprouted freely over their length and breadth. This apparently decorative feature was intended for defense. From a distance, the palace seemed to be a grove tended by a careful landscape artist. The dark green color was not unattractive, but any contact with the plants or—still worse—any tasting of these berries would bring fever, constant diarrhea, and a sleep from which one never awoke. That is to say, the victim's eyelids would remain hermetically sealed even as the rest of the senses continued to operate. Some parts of the structure were covered by these vines to a height of fifty meters, while others remained naked in their gray or reddish colors as if those walls had stood for centuries. What was most marvelous was that the vegetation constituted a medical resource, too. The imperial doctors stationed there could repair scars and cure some forms of tooth decay with potions made from the same material that, in the hands of novices or assassins, would prove fatal.

When Clock entered the castle, without having passed through any gate, only a series of linked paths, a Tibetan girl was singing while a musician accompanied her with the sweet sounds of a flute. Clock's nose made out, among various competing smells, the stubborn odor of cod. And indeed, in the great kitchen of the castle a delicious dinner was being prepared for the participants in the game and the soldiers who had fulfilled their duty of capturing the mechanic.

In the kitchen, cooks were slicing the cod into chunks. Skillfully, they shaped fine strips of ginger. The chef shouted orders like an engineer supervising the construction of a drawbridge. Mushrooms, bamboo shoots, onions. In one corner, a worker was peeling sweet potatoes.

"Hey, you, roll up the ginger and the mushrooms in that fish!"

"You over there, corn oil! Where's the oil, I want to know!"

A famous *sheng* player coaxed melodies out of that woodwind as if all this had nothing to do with him—because it had nothing to do with him. Strangely, the cook in charge of beating egg whites did so with great efficiency but without the noise of his actions interfering with any melody. He poured cornmeal into the eggs as if he could hear, in its fall, an integral part of the harmony.

The sizzle of the frying pans, the sound of each roll being pulled out one at a time, golden brown and dripping, all seemed to make up part of the imperial orchestra. The finishing touch came from the percussion section; as red sauce in a bowl was mixed with a bit of sugar and vinegar, salt, and broth, the sounds of colliding wood, porcelain, and metal did justice to those of musical compositions.

"Hey, more seasoning in that hot pan! The rolls, the rolls!" the chef ordered like a vocalist singing out of tune. "Sesame oil on the griddle, now!"

But those commands were completely unnecessary, because the cooks carried out their duties with apparent art, pleasure, and sometimes even joy.

"Where are the damn boiled sweet potatoes? Okay, good. Good. No, over there. . . . Okay, now, that's it!"

When all was ready, color flowed back into the chef's visage. He wiped off the sweat with a white linen cloth and smiled for the first time. The kitchen workers sprinkled cilantro over the dozens of serving platters.

Panwok, as the director of this symphony of cooks was named, began to congratulate everyone with a solemn speech that included tales of the daring fishermen who had caught the cod in waters off Madagascar and those other travelers who had dug tubers in southern Africa so as to transplant and cultivate them in the area around the magnificent fortress. The stories seemed exaggerated, but the listeners accepted them without protest so as not to interrupt. The emperor's representative stepped into the kitchen's entryway, and Panwok began to reprise for his benefit the story of the fishermen's crusade to the isle of lemurs. For the benefit of all, the representative told him to be quiet and serve the food quickly.

• • •

Clock had been treated with care and respect. He had been bathed in a tub full of flowers by three well-dressed ladies but had resisted any temptations because they carried out their task with a degree of brusqueness or coldness. Or perhaps he was just very tired? Now, here he was awaiting the meal in the ample dining hall. A series of delicate metallic poles and crosspieces, perhaps of bronze, kept the area free of ivy, which grew only within spaces defined by thin panels of onyx and ebony. In an upper gallery, as if suspended in air, were a series of bays with tall glass windows that reached to the roof. At the back of the room was a small separate area also protected behind glass.

At the far end of the great hall, seated in a small area set off by a curtain made of flat panes of glass, were some of the participants in the ceremonial game that Clock had witnessed a few hours before. They were having a lively conversation, and the youngest among them seemed the most amused. His exquisite indigo uniform bore streaks and patches of dirt, but this did not seem to bother him. Rather, he wore them like decorations of honor.

At the tables nearest to the time-mechanic, meanwhile, sat men in orange robes, likewise stained with dirt. He realized they were the monks who had also participated in the unusual rite. They ate gratefully and without any breach of etiquette. He approached them and asked the significance of the simulation he had observed.

"It is called Banqiú. This was how the Immortal Souls in the Ts'sai Valley amused themselves," one of the Buddhist monks explained.

General Huen-wen approached Clock and asked him the questions that courtesy required.

"How did you find the meal?"

"It was excellent. There must be a whole army of slaves behind such ambrosia."

"An orchestra, better put. A battalion of virtuosos. And yet, you must have found that it contained nothing to excess."

"Indeed that is so. Lovely flavors, but with no need to show off."

"Excess kills more efficiently than swords."

"Some sage must be the author of that phrase."

"The Emperor."

“And where is that honorable sovereign?”

“Right there,” the General said, pointing toward the glass curtain through which the group of men in clothing the color of the mid-afternoon sky could be seen. Even though Clock had suspected the supreme ruler might among the group, he displayed surprise.

“Could he be the one bearing the most decorations of soil on his uniform?”

“That is he. One of his watchwords says, “Play as if today were the final day. Fight as if it were the last day. Because in fact, it is.”

BIG LEAGUES

Salvador Fleján
(Venezuela)

Salvador Fleján, (Caracas, 1966), is a graduate in language and literature of the Universidad Central de Venezuela, the winner of several prizes for fiction, and a judge in prestigious literary contests. He is the author of four collections of stories and creative nonfiction—Intriga en el Car Wash (2006), Miniaturas salvajes (2012), Ruedalibre (2014), and Tardes felices (2016)—and has been published widely in newspapers, magazines, and anthologies in Venezuela and abroad. His regular column about events of daily life is featured in the Caracas political weekly Quinto Día. He is working on his first novel.

It ain't over till it's over.

—YOGI BERRA

To me, taking pride in a son because he inherits his grandmother's blue eyes or strings together sentences at eighteen months is as foolish as taking pleasure in a neighbor's winning the lottery.

Yesterday at my nephew's birthday party I heard a talented child recite poems and pluck out tunes on the *cuatro*. That was when I realized something that both surprised and saddened me: behind those kinds of kids there's always a proud, dimwit parent who takes on undeserved airs. My story is different, as you will see, though you'll draw your own conclusions.

• • •

Just a glance at my Keny's chest and arms when he turned ten was enough to set anybody to making calculations. To dreaming, at least a little. He looked like a mini-Hercules. It was so striking that his teacher and my wife were worried. But not me. Maybe his size was a bad omen, given my family history, but it wasn't the "elephantitis" that Rosalía was afraid of.

By then I knew my son was born with the attributes, though, in truth, I had known it for a while. When I say "attributes," I mean what you need to be somebody in this country: a good arm, power, and speed in the legs. The rest—except for intelligence—can be taught in any *rookie league*.

Keny, like my uncle and my brother, was born with these aptitudes. In my family, that privilege has exacted a high price.

Calixto, my father's brother, had an inborn talent for baseball, a talent he was far from knowing he possessed. He never played professionally. His best afternoons of *la pelota* came in industrial league tournaments, on fields without grass or spectators. My uncle was a swamp orchid, a stray talent. He had opportunity aplenty, but it wasn't going to happen for Calixto unless the owner of the Baltimore Orioles himself came begging with contract in hand. When someone is born to be a worker, what can you do? I don't blame Calixto. That was a different time, and my uncle—fine man that he was—preferred the tranquil security of a Water and Sewer

Department pension to the dizzying demands of a multiyear contract. At fifty-three, standing in line at the bank to cash his retirement check, he had a heart attack.

* * *

With my brother, things were different, though believe me I would have preferred otherwise. In the early 1960s he signed with a professional Venezuelan team, a short-lived franchise, as it turned out. When they signed him he was seventeen, six foot three, and very sure of his prospects. He was a handsome guy, too, and with such natural gifts plus an aversion to school, devoting himself to baseball was one of the few reasonable decisions he ever made.

Eleazar played two seasons in the Venezuelan circuit. The term "tore up the league" was never more appropriate. Don't ask me for statistics or averages, because numbers don't interest me, but I can tell you what everyone remembers, which is that he led in several different offensive categories and was a serious threat to break a number of hallowed records.

The smell of fresh blood inevitably attracted the hyenas.

The scouts' reports indicated that a gem of many carats had been found in a mine with an unpronounceable name. Eleazar had everything he needed. Or almost. What happened to him is still shrouded in mystery, known only within the family, but there's no reason to keep it secret anymore. Some say he couldn't handle the pressure. I'd like to see them try! Few could have withstood it. My brother didn't even finish high school, but he was demolishing the pitches of imported players. My poor brother, just another kid from San Juan parish, was suddenly being pursued by the most important major league teams.

Forty years ago, things were more pastoral, weren't they, in baseball's so-called romantic age? Let me tell you something about the romantic age—it never existed. The kids today have it a lot easier. The big teams even have psychologists that help the youngsters survive their millions of dollars. The difference between baseball then and baseball now is not romanticism, but the number of zeroes to the right of the salaries. All the rest is the same business as ever. A business with wolves and sheep.

Our house in La Pastora filled with wolves. There were packs of scouts coming and going. Every one of them tried to bribe the old man with amazing offers. My father, who was poor but not stupid, dodged them with evasive responses and inscrutable smiles. The scramble went on until El Loco Torres, a family friend, proposed the solution.

"Listen, Rafael," he told my father as they sat together in the kitchen. "Horses are no good for barbecue. They're very pretty, but all they do is eat and shit. If you keep waiting, not even a bush league team is going to make an offer. What we need is an auction, and we need to do it before he's past his prime."

El Loco's solution was neither evil nor misguided. It was logical. Every time Eleazar opened the refrigerator, the family budget tottered. His salary with the local team was nothing to brag about, and Papa's wages weren't enough to supply the nutritional needs of a mammoth like him. And he'd turned twenty, the age by which a ballplayer either is on the fast track or never will be.

Things had to be done the American way, El Loco said. That meant staging a *trayao*.

I remember the tryout, held on a Sunday morning in the University Stadium. The sun bouncing off the stands painted the outfield grass an emerald tone I haven't seen since—the green of an isolated, melancholy bay, accentuated by the silence of the empty stadium.

El Loco had taken care of all the details: inviting the scouts (or, really, disinviting those we didn't want), securing the batting cage and other equipment, coming up with some guys to help out on the field. Even a cooler full of beers was waiting for the signing ceremony. And everything would have gone like clockwork except for an event that El Loco didn't foresee or just couldn't imagine. I was sitting in the stands, on the right side just behind first base, watching him slowly rubbing a bat. It was a small bat and strangely shaped. I couldn't tell whether he was wiping it clean or asking it to grant him a wish.

* * *

The wish was granted two hours later than the scheduled time. Eleazar showed up after a night on the town, more sleep-deprived than drunk, singing a *guaracha*. He didn't offer greetings, and he didn't apologize. My dad and El Loco were both red-faced with shame. The only scouts remaining were Mr. Mosley of the Yankees and a short guy in a panama hat who represented the White Sox. The rest had refused to tolerate the insult and were long gone. I don't know how El Loco managed to convince these two to stay and take a look. I think the cold beers in the cooler helped make his words more eloquent and persuasive.

Eleazar ducked into the *dogao* and came back five minutes later, in uniform and with a bat on his shoulder. Watching him stride to the batting cage, no one would have imagined he had a night of rum and merengue on his back.

When he stood at the plate I thought he was going to melt from one minute to the next. To be out there under the blazing noonday sun was just short of suicide. His grip on the bat looked tentative and his swings lethargic, but the ringing rhythm of bat meeting ball dissolved this false impression. It was a staccato series of dull, concave sounds, like a horse galloping on a concrete floor.

The scouts were more interested in grabbing a last beer out of the cooler than in what was happening on the field, but that music managed to grab their attention.

With each crack of the bat, the expressions on their faces—like those of my father and El Loco—evolved from incredulity to amazement to greed. El Loco knew this was Eleazar's only chance to show off his talents, so he quickly ordered up another bucket of balls. The ones that didn't go tamely into the centerfield stands went whistling past the ears of the guy on the mound.

As a counterpoint, or maybe an anticlimax, El Loco sent Eleazar out to third base to take grounders. He looked a little clumsy with the glove, as if he didn't quite know what he was doing out there. His body needed two quarts of water or eight hours' sleep or both at once. But he did show off a strong and well-trained arm that sent sand flying off the mitt of the guy on first taking the throws. Testing the speed of Eleazar's legs was a crime that El Loco didn't dare commit. Things had gone well enough not to tempt fate any further.

The contest between the scouts was strange.

Or so I thought when Mr. Mosley abandoned ship. The bids were reaching the level of offers for a Ming vase, but then the New York scout said wearily, "Gentlemen, that's enough." Maybe the Yankees' finances were in disrepair just then, though probably not. Maybe, though I didn't think of this till later, the gringo had a premonition.

But the White Sox rep felt differently. A couple of years in the beginners' league, he thought, would perform the miracle of turning coal to diamond. As this hope turned to certainty, he offered sixty thousand dollars for a signing bonus—a notorious sum, a record for that day and age. When it was all done, my father beamed as if an invisible hand were stroking his back. El Loco performed like a lawyer with a degree from Yale. The vehemence with which he argued over the bonus, clauses, and perks was something to see.

For reasons that I don't know how to explain, I had the feeling that things would change forever from that day on. In return for his sweat, Eleazar asked only for a new-model

Buick, which he totaled within a month. The old man invested the rest of the money, a sizable sum, in a house on the Avenida Páez and the store he presided over till his death.

* * *

In their effort to convert my brother into a true ballplayer, the White Sox assigned him to a Double-A league in the Midwest. The team's training camp was a former air force base turned sports complex. All around stretched the proverbial amber waves of grain.

My brother quickly revealed himself to be the best of the bunch, with his batting as the principal evidence. In the babel of accents from the varied shores of the Caribbean, his *vale* and *carajo* began to stand out. Soon the general manager showed up to follow his tape-measure drives in person, attracted by the idea of a high-yield, low-cost third baseman.

At home we harbored the hope that Eleazar would be called up at any moment. To tell the truth, all our hopes were riding on that idea. Many of the perks that El Loco had negotiated were conditioned on that eventuality. Seeing Eleazar become a big-league player went from being a family dream to a sort of underground raffle in which my brother was the only ticket we had.

But something happened.

One night of monotony and raging hormones, Eleazar escaped from the concentration camp without notifying his manager. The team had returned from a road trip of three games in Omaha, and everybody was tired and bored. All except my brother, who dreamed of a cold beer, or preferably several.

The nearest town was forty-five minutes away at a brisk walk. Eleazar must have been plenty thirsty, because it took him only half an hour to get from the sports complex to the first bar he could find. When he entered, all eyes turned toward him with a blend of surprise and distaste. Eleazar was neither black nor white. He had some Indian features, but his face also preserved the traces of some rough Basque ancestor lost in our twisted family tree. I suppose the local parishioners were just not ready for that confusion of races, for so much collision of worlds.

It took fifteen minutes for the police to arrive. To their surprise, what they found did not match the urgency of the summons. Eleazar was seated on the jukebox, though he seemed more to be levitating above it. His hair was in disarray and his face expressed the peacefulness and fatalism of a vagrant bumming a cigarette. The rest of the picture was more alarming: three plump farmers scattered about the floor, broken chairs, bloodstains, and the bar owner with shotgun in hand.

One of the team's investors happened to be a senator from the state of North Dakota. This coincidence made it possible for Eleazar to step off a plane the next day in Caracas. Left behind were some one-sided charges of assault and battery and the applause of Comiskey Park.

• • •

A few local sportswriters were merciful enough to concoct a story involving homesickness, a longing for Venezuelan food, and a mother who was unwell. I suppose such sophisms were also part of the romantic era.

What happened after that is more or less well known. That journalistic charity allowed my brother to add one more year of Venezuelan professional ball to his career, though I think the word "career" is excessive, because he didn't even play out the season. Little by little, partying and drink ate away at his batting average and his body.

I don't know whether the team's owner got fed up, or whether he took pity on Eleazar, but either way, the firing was private and discreet. The owner summoned Eleazar to his office, and his final words were, "It's such a shame, buddy. You look more like a boxer than a ballplayer, you know?"

• • •

In the blink of an eye, that replica of Greek god turned into a skinny, hunched scarecrow, a cruel nightmare image of what my brother used to be. At home, no one talked about baseball anymore. Eleazar found it harder and harder to stay sober. When he didn't take off for long periods, he spent hours sitting on the porch, drunk. His eyes had gone bleary and vacant, seemingly in search of some horizon he could never locate again.

The respect and admiration I'd once felt for my brother were gradually transformed into a mix of compassion, disgust, and disappointment. Papa was the only one to watch out for him and protect him as much as he was able. Really, though, there wasn't much he could do. Toward the end, something would drive Eleazar out of the house every night. Maybe he thought he was fleeing the tedium of that former air force base.

One night he left and never came back.

At first we didn't realize how long he'd been gone. We'd gotten used to him in the way you get used to an old or useless piece of furniture, or a ghost. But something told my father this last flight from home was different, or, at least, that his return was delayed well past the usual limits. Somebody reported seeing him walking along the shoulder of a highway in dirty, tattered clothes. Somebody else spotted him on the steps of a church, begging. Myself, I thought I saw him peeking in my window one night, but maybe that was a dream. Anyway, it was him, and he looked clean and his clothes were intact. He'd put on some weight, and his eyes had their old liveliness back. What I can remember best is his smile, a strange one, as if he weren't really smiling, but then again, he was. I told my father, but he didn't believe me. Maybe it was better that way. Papa went out every day in search of him, armed with those false clues. Though I'm having trouble lately recalling details, I don't remember ever seeing the old man come back discouraged or defeated. He always had fresh reports of sightings that renewed his hopes.

When they called us with the news that Eleazar had been run over by a truck, I felt this was already old news, as if we were being brought up to date on something that had happened quite a long time before. I think Eleazar was dead from the moment the White Sox put him on that plane for home.

• • •

My son's signing was neither good nor bad in itself. It all depends how you look at it. Eight hundred thousand dollars was nothing to sneeze at in the era when he was signed. But I don't think it was fair price, either, for a left-handed pitcher with the control Keny displayed at the age of sixteen.

That sum, now that I think about it, didn't do much honor to the innumerable Sunday afternoons I spent sitting on grimy benches with the nails sticking out, pretending I was in a VIP box in Yankee Stadium. Nobody said so out loud, but all of us there on those benches knew this was the price we had to pay, and we all knew it was just a question of time. We knew our buds were going to bloom. We knew they wouldn't get stunted at a height of five foot seven, damned forevermore. We knew they wouldn't get some girl pregnant. We knew.

• • •

After the Astros signed Keny, my old coworkers at the ministry—the few I was still in touch with—started greeting me with expressions suspended between amazement and envy.

Ah, the envy! Who was it that said envy is skinny because it never eats, only bites? That is sure the truth. And so Venezuelan, too, my God. When news of the signing came out in the papers, one of the first to call to offer his support was a former boss of mine, a tyrant who had made life impossible. Since I don't hold grudges, I accepted his invitation to have lunch. I knew that his son had turned out to be a slacker and a pothead—everybody in the ministry knew that. I'm nobody to be making judgments about others, but after this guy offered me his pained congratulations and then began slinging barbed comments like "what matters isn't getting there but staying there" and "this kid inherited *everything* from his uncle," I couldn't take any more. With this Salieri I decided to call a spadc a spade.

"Look," I said, "Maybe my boy will only last two days in the major leagues. Maybe he's inherited a lot from his uncle. Anything is possible. But tell me something. I know where your son got his laziness—from you. But his taste for weed, which side of the family did that come from?

• • •

Keny whizzed through the minors as fast as you could take a breath. Within a year he'd jumped from an instructional rookie league to the Triple-A farm team in Norfolk. His record of 7–3 with an ERA of 1.59 showed that he was going to break the curse that hovered over our family, for good and all. Halfway through the year, the general manager was ready to call him up to the big-league club, but the manager at Norfolk was more judicious. The rookie still needed to polish a few things about his pitching mechanics, he said.

When Keny came home for the winter break, I was struck by the equanimity with which he took everything. This didn't reassure me, but the opposite. He was neither happy nor sad, neither enthusiastic nor apathetic. In words that were more or less devoid of emotion, he told us that, assuming things went on as they'd been going, he'd be on the Astros' forty-man roster the next year. I could never understand that boy. Just a step away from glory, an inch from emerging from the herd into the spotlight, and he sounded like he was being sent to harvest crops on a plantation. But before he left for Virginia, Keny told me the problem. It was as obvious as it was simple.

"I've never liked baseball, Papa. I'm doing all this for you."

Right then I didn't know how to fully appreciate those words, though now I do. Now I understand why my son agreed to go along with the plan of "less school, more stadium" that I had laid out for him since he was little. I never demanded good grades in chemistry or physics, only on the field. He always knew that what would make me happy would be seeing our name in letters across his back, not on an academic diploma.

• • •

Halfway through the season, Keny hurt his pitching arm.

When that happened, my boy was rated as the organization's A-1 prospect. He was undefeated after eight starts and was the talk of the league. No other pitcher in Norfolk's history, whether righty or lefty, had achieved such a record in his second year. Two days before the injury, the call-up order from the big club was sitting on the manager's desk.

Keny never knew.

The injury itself was not all that serious. A bone spur on the elbow is as common among pitchers as the habit of putting saliva on the ball. The operation and the rehab were routine; the club had a doctor who specialized in that kind of surgery.

Still, Keny's return to the Norfolk rotation was not completely satisfactory. His performance had deteriorated slightly.

He'd lost a little off his fastball, not much, but enough to worry the general manager.

When my son called to say his contract had been sold to a team in Taiwan, what he really wanted was permission to come home to Caracas. I think I heard him crying on the other end of the line, or maybe the connection was bad. I adlibbed a speech about perseverance and other such nonsense. At some point I cried, too. Both of us knew he was never going to wear a big-league uniform again.

What happened after that I've had to piece together out of loose ends, half-truths, and my own imagination.

The team that bought Keny's contract was called the Bears, or maybe Elephants, or maybe even Coyotes, if they have coyotes in that part of the world. Whatever, it was one of the strongest teams in the league—and the main target of the Taiwanese gambling mafia.

In Taiwan, Keny recovered his form. Though I think he'd never really lost it, I think what he lost was his confidence, and for a pitcher that's a serious thing. In his first two starts in Taiwan, he was simply unhittable. He demonstrated his old control and velocity, with the radar gun clocking him at up to 98 miles per hour. His pitches came in sharp and on the corners, intimidating for batters who aren't so tall. And Taiwan, of course, is no land of giants.

One night when the summer monsoon was drenching the streets of Taipei, Keny received a proposition. The proposition was backed up by two irrefutable arguments: a bag stuffed with Taiwan dollars and a threat.

It didn't take Keny long to get the picture. He tried to reason with them, but in vain. The mafia—Taiwanese, Italian, or Venezuelan—always tries the carrot first. The emissaries, as if they knew past, present, and future by heart, dropped the bag on his bed. Each put a hand on his shoulder and told him, "You losing tomorrow."

That ungrammatical sentence plunged him into uncertainty and panic. His first impulse was to go find the manager of the team and announce that he was quitting. He didn't do it. Instead, I got a harrowing call at two a.m.

That was the last time I talked with my son.

* * *

I spent the insurance money on a mausoleum in the Cementerio del Este. It's made of white marble, in the best part of the cemetery. It's beautiful, it really is. An homage to my boy that I wanted to make. I go every Sunday and, though I don't pray, I spend hours in front of a picture that I had them seal onto the tombstone. He's twelve years old, in a baseball uniform, and his eyes are translucent and stern.

Sometimes I think (and other times I'm sure) that instead of sitting on marble tiles I'm back on the benches full of nails and grime, where I used to sit and wait and dream.

HOW TOMBOY MARÍA LEARNED SHE COULD FLY

Daniel Ernesto Reyes Germán
(Dominican Republic)

Daniel Reyes Germán (Santo Domingo, 1988) writes under his own name and under the pseudonym Daniel Kinger. He studied filmmaking at the Universidad Autónoma de Santo Domingo and has won several Dominican literary prizes, including the second prize in the Primer Concurso de Cuentos sobre Beisbol (2008) and second, third, and fourth prizes in the Fundación Juan Bosch's 100 Años en 100 Palabras (2010). He also writes and illustrates stories for children and young adults.

The ant that grows wings is the one that goes astray.

— POPULAR SAYING

I've got rhythm, I've got swing, I play ball like anything.

— MERENGUE LYRIC

On its way from the capital to Los Llanos, the Mella Highway passes through a series of cane fields. When you reach signpost number who-knows-what, you can catch a glimpse of the town of San Luis. You can see the sugarcane railway, the oxen pulling their heavy loads, and the cane cutters with dark skin and brown-sugar souls, machetes in hand, sharp blades in constant twisting motion, right to left, right to left, chopping at the green foliage that seems to glow and pant in the heat. You may feel you're breathing through a vat full of sugar, the best definition of a sweet smell. There, to the east of steamy Santo Domingo, is Josefina's house.

She's having labor pains.

"Where's my pregnant lady?" asks a woman with a hint of smile. She is directed to a bedroom. She's the midwife, everyone calls her La Matrona. As fate will have it, the *señora* Josefina Pierre gives birth to a girl.

Josefina had her daughter the regular way, in her own home and without complications. Though she was Catholic more by upbringing than by belief, that was enough to provide the child a name: María del Carmen. María del Carmen Paúl Pierre. Both parents were of Haitian descent.

Every day, María del Carmen walked to the country schoolhouse carrying a cane-leaf chair over her head. The chair was both her seat in the classroom and the weapon she wielded in the fights she got into, even at that age. She loved busting heads. Of course she was sent home in the company of a teacher, but that did not get her punished. The neighbors said her parents spoiled her, overly supportive as they were. María del Carmen Paúl Pierre was lively and smart. Her body was striking and exotic for her years: black, tall, and thin with a long, willowy spine, her kinky hair braided and tied with red ribbons. Her parents tried to hide her signs of masculinity, which disappeared anyway as she turned adolescent and adult. She exuded natural leadership; if you were a child her age, you both feared her and wanted to follow her. But in the environment in which she lived, her only outlet was to prance, tease, fight, and get into trouble, provoking complaints from teachers, relatives, friends, classmates, and neighbors.

One fine day, the school sent a counselor to give María del Carmen's parents some advice. In the cramped parlor of their house, they waited expectantly for what he had to say.

"The girl has a lot of energy, she's hyperactive," he said. "The best thing would be for her to take on some kind of activity or project. Maybe some kind of sport—something to get all the bad stuff out of her head. You know what they say," the counselor added with the dispassionate calm of a psychologist, "An idle mind is the devil's workshop."

"She washes dishes and sometimes she goes with me to the river to do the clothes," her mother offered without much hope.

"That's not enough. She needs an activity that requires more energy, time, and effort. If I may say so, your daughter is very jumpy. It's almost as if she were trying to fly, that's the feeling I get, and nothing good can come of that." The teacher stood up, his lips seeming to offer a silent prayer that came from deep inside. "As my folks used to put it," he added, "'The ant that grows wings is the one that goes astray.' Those old sayings don't lie."

What he recommended was a little league that held its games on the ball field at the edge of the village. He pointed that way with his chin, as if he were trying to plant a kiss on the wind. Unable to come up with any reasons for delay, Josefina took María del Carmen by the arm and led her to the site that everyone called the *play,* which was baking under the unforgiving sun of a cloudless day.

The arrival of the unlikely visitors awakened universal curiosity on the *play*. Throwing arms stopped in midair, bats did not swing, gloves did not reach out to catch balls in flight. One such ball raised a cloud of dust as it collided with the ground. Craning their necks to the point of injury, everyone stared at the pair of females who shyly stepped onto the green grass in search of the coach.

"How do I sign her up?" Josefina blurted out, taking the bull by the horns.

"First of all, ma'am, we take only boys. There isn't any girls' league."

A few boys laughed, though if María del Carmen were to find them outside the ball field she would surely make them pay, one by one. The coach shushed them. He was a tall, ordinary man, dressed no better than a scarecrow, with a dried-out face like a cashew nut.

"It's doctor's orders," Josefina lied, irreverent and confident. "She needs to be here."

The manager hesitated a moment and noted that María looked to be the right size to play third base, where he needed someone to round out his team. He picked up a notebook, gave the strange pair another once-over, and asked, "Does this little piece of work have a name?"

"She's María del Carmen Paúl Pierre."

The coach wrote this down and told her to run a few laps to warm up. He told her mother, "We'll give her a tryout to see if she's got what it takes." His tone was not lacking in innuendo. "When practice is over we'll send her home to you."

María del Carmen heard him and thought, "I'm no message to send and no soldier to give orders to."

The manager handed her a bat and watched as she assumed her stance. "She's got something," he thought. He told his best pitcher to throw a fastball by her.

Some more boys laughed, and she glanced at them just long enough to memorize their faces. Then she swung and made contact with the ball. It was a *rolling*, but well hit, so the manager said, "Okay Tomboy María. Let's see how you field." And he spit, grinding the toe of his shoe over the saliva that turned the dirt to mud.

From then on she was not María del Carmen Paúl Pierre. Everyone called her Tomboy María.

When she got home that afternoon, all the neighborhood kids wanted to hear how she had done. Everyone knew about the morning's visit from the school and her being sent to join the league. She ducked inside just long enough to grab the necessities for stickball. The usual odds and ends of players took turns at bat and in the field. It wasn't long before the game expanded to include whole teams, and variations were added: bases made of old license plates, home run derbies, and more. United by their fever for baseball, the children would play until the sun sank below the horizon.

* * *

"Everything had better go right, or I'm going to kick your asses. You're a bunch of lazy clowns, and if I have to tell anybody anything twice, he better be ready for what I do next. I'm not going all the way there to get shown up or to lose, especially on somebody else's turf. And another thing: get the money together. You know the price of the round trip, so don't play dumb like you never heard about it. We're leaving at four a.m., on the dot, American time. That's it. Now get going," he ordered. "I want to see you sweat. Except you, Tomboy María. I have something to discuss with you."

María's heart skipped a beat, her pulse stopped, she didn't breathe. For a few seconds she froze in fright.

"Coach, I'll bring the cash tomorrow, when my father gets paid," she stammered, dropping her eyes and wringing her hands together, awakening the man's compassion.

"No, that's not it." He hesitated for a moment like a bearer of bad news. "The thing is, you can't go. The league is for boys. You're not allowed."

He spoke to her more courteously than usual, as if it really did hurt him to say this. Still he did not stray far from his usual brusqueness. "I'm sorry, I really am. Tell that to Doña Josefina, so she'll know."

Tomboy María nodded reluctantly. She climbed up on the bleachers and squatted there. All the anger she had bottled up to avoid causing problems in the league threatened to come pouring out. She remembered the moments when she was the idol of everyone watching in the *play*. Her eyes reddened and tears welled up in her chest, like when she got in fights at school. Although she felt humiliated, degraded, she couldn't show weakness. She thought she was the best player on the team, and she wasn't wrong. She remembered her recurrent dream of flying alongside a column of ants after a fierce downpour. The day she woke up in terror from the first of those dreams, her mother took her small head between her breasts and said, "Joseph in the Bible dreamed of flying, and he ended up the leader of his people. The next time you dream this, concentrate on your goals." That's what she said, more or less, though not in those exact words. Tomboy María decided that playing baseball was her greatest and most longed-for desire.

When practice was over, all the boys headed for home. Tomboy María looked at the ones who had laughed at her when she first appeared. Now she had nothing to lose. The news that she couldn't go on the trip and show off all she had accomplished wounded the innermost corners of her soul.

"So what is it?" she shouted. "Do I have shit on my face? Do I look like some kind of clown?" She was going to give each of them what they deserved. But she controlled herself, again thinking about the consequences of her actions. It was more important to stay in the league than to break a few heads and give the boys the thrashing they deserved. She held onto the vague hope of coming back from a championship series, someday, with the gold medals she had imagined during stifling sleepless nights. She turned around and headed home, leaving the boys shocked at the gestures she made for them to remember her by. She loved baseball more than she loved busting heads. Though it was hard for her to believe sometimes, she felt so good simply because she could run faster, swing harder, steal more bases, and catch with more precision than the rest. A sense of superiority was what her soul needed most.

Still, Tomboy María could not hide her sadness when she got home. She came in with her head hanging. Her mother had been waiting for something like this to happen. It was to be expected. But she asked, putting down the broom, "What's going on?"

"They won't let me go play in a game between provinces because I'm a girl," María said between sobs.

"Don't worry, baby, I'll go talk with the coach."

Josefina sat her daughter down in the rocking chair and told her not to move from the spot, that she'd be back soon. She went out the door with a determined air and disappeared among the curves of the road.

"I can't do anything for your daughter," the coach said. "It makes me feel bad too. She's a good player, but she's a girl. Anyway, we can get by without her."

That annoyed Josefina all the more.

"My daughter's the best player," she said with swelling anger. "Why don't you pick out your best boy player and this afternoon we'll pit them against each other, so you can see." Josefina had a dark kerchief tied around her head, hiding the gray of her hair. She wore a cream-colored housedress, immaculately clean. On her feet were a pair of yellowed samurai sandals, dry and cracked. This challenge would show that she was right. The coach accepted. But first he warned, "It won't win her permission to go on the trip." He punctuated the statement with a jab of his index finger, trying to hold his own.

"But it will give her back her dignity," Josefina whispered into the air while turning her back to hide her impotence. She remained proud of her determination.

• • •

Hours later, Tomboy María was drawing a pair of wings on her shoulder. This, from her point of view, conferred even more talent on her arms, so she could swing harder and fulfill her dreams.

"Those who believe in you, Lord, will never be ashamed, Amen." And she headed for the challenge, fulfilling her duty.

In spite of her great accomplishments as a player, Tomboy María never found a place in her town or her society. The years went by, doing what they do, inscribing lines on her face and, even more so, putting her physical attributes on display, turning her into a blossoming teenage girl. When she was eighteen she met Miguel Luí, an elegant and well-mannered plowman whose strong biceps guided oxen through the endless fields of cane. He was tall and dark with flashing eyes. They fell deeply in love. They conceived a boy whom they named Miguel Ángel Luí Paúl.

"He's going to be a ballplayer," said the new mother in a wisp of a voice, with tears in her eyes as she beheld the gasping baby in her lap.

After a moment of complete silence, while the baby gathered breath to erupt into cries, Miguel said, "María, I have to go the capital to find work." He said it baldly, without beating around the bush. She looked him in the eyes while she rocked and tried to calm the baby. It was obvious that he was leaving for good. A man who flees from such situations is worthless and a coward, she thought. He was in debt even for the candles he lit to the Virgin and his prayers to the saints, which was to say that if indulgences were still for sale he'd buy them with borrowed money, and if Jesus came back and found him in such a state, He would leave him to his tears here on earth.

For extended periods, mother and baby had to live on meat that was on the edge of spoiling for lack of electricity.

People called it fishy meat because of its unique and penetrating smell, like that of a stinking sea. It took no great powers of analysis to see that Miguel Luí wasn't coming back. He was a weak-willed man, the neighbors told María del Carmen, but she received these comments with an unseeing and complacent smile. Miguel Luí did not want to live in such a degrading situation anymore. That's why he wasn't coming back.

• • •

It has been argued that time does not exist, that for lack of legs it can neither stand still nor run. So, let's just say that Miguel Ángel's age increased, Miguel Ángel the son of Tomboy María—that now he was no longer a child in diapers but a strapping youth who helped his mother with the chores. He gathered wood for the fire and charcoal for the stove, he carried heavy sacks of provisions from the small plot of land to the small house. The village of San Luis, despite its backward condition, is only an hour from the capital by bus. So María del Carmen could travel to work in the city during the day.

Later, after Tomboy María's death, a villager named Fernando would tell how he drove a National Brewery truck there in the capital and how he came to meet her at a certain place on the road, pointing vaguely with his fingers. "So I was driving, you know," he said with some pride, "and I was always horny as a young man. I'd stopped by the monument that's famous for these things, you know, to look for a 'social worker,' the girls that sold a good time. One day the pimp told me that, since I was a special customer, he had something new for me. Into the passenger seat climbed a black girl who was something to write home about. I was hung over like you wouldn't believe, and anyway it was pretty dark for recognizing faces. But she recognized me."

"Fernando?" she asked, surprised.

"If you say so," he answered, not understanding what this was about. When he turned on the light in the cabin of the truck, he saw a sorrowful face swollen with tears. Even in the dim light he could tell she was ashamed.

"Don't tell anybody, Fernando, I beg you," she said. "I'll do whatever you want."Shocked, he pulled some coins out of his pocket and gave them to her. "Go," he said. "Tell the pimp I chickened out. Tomorrow come by my place and I'll get you an honest job at the brewery."

The next day she did. Fernando took her to the brewery and managed to get her a cleaning job. Weekends she worked extra hours. But later he discovered that she had met another trucker there, and she went to bed for money—with him and others who would pay.

When Fernando learned what she was doing, he arranged to see her alone and advise her against this behavior. She told him she needed the money to send her son to Puerto Rico, where there were important big league representatives scouting the young players. When she finished washing Fernando's clothes, she said to him, "I live for my son now. We went through a lot together, and what I want for him now is to be what I could never be."

She was not well, you could tell it from her yellowish eyes and darkened skin. Fernando advised her to go the hospital for a checkup, but she wouldn't do it, not until later, when they discovered the illness that would take her life.

• • •

"Mama, I need a pair of cleats. They lent me these so I could run faster, and they work, but I want a pair of my own. And I need a metal bat for practicing on my own, and some yellow baseballs. An equipment bag and a helmet. . . ."

Miguel Ángel went on asking for things as if he were reading a speech.

Tomboy María's head was spinning. A dull, internal throbbing punctuated her thoughts. She was getting weaker every day, with less strength to go on, but she had to be there for her son, to see him fulfill his dreams and those she'd been unable to achieve as a child. She had gotten together the money for his travel and accommodation in Puerto Rico, where the best contracts could be signed. This was Miguel Ángel's and Tomboy María's dream. They couldn't wait for the day to arrive.

"Don't worry, Mama, I'm going to shine. I'm going to do it. I'm going to stand out, to fly the way you used to do. Your efforts won't be in vain. Look." And his lifted up his t-shirt, showing his bare chest. "I had two wings tattooed, and your name, Mama, look at it, the guy in the grocery did it in honor of you. When I come back here signed, with all those dollars, I'll pay you back for everything you've done for me." When he didn't get the response he'd expected, he quickly pulled the shirt down again.

"Son, all I want is to see you alive and healthy. If God grants that I get to see you signed, I won't complain."

They both smiled, neither meeting the other's eyes. She set the table and he spoke with feeling, as if savoring that moment. Tomboy María was lying, but her son didn't believe her anyway. Everyone in the neighborhood knew that she'd give her life to see her son signed. Word of his tryout circulated after she let it slip to one of the truckers. Everybody knew what was afoot.

* * *

Amid all the sacrifices she was compelled to make, María remembered the old saying that life was lived by fire and blood, and she understood. Miguel Ángel went to Puerto Rico and came back with a contract, but he had to give the news to his mother in the morgue. She died from a venereal disease caught from one of the truckers. They say that he did what she had done when she wasn't allowed to go and play in the interprovincial game, that he painted wings on his bat and prayed. They say that when he saw his mother in the coffin he told her this story as if she could hear it. He sat next to the corpse, sitting and swaying like a man under a spell. And he repeated. "Mama grew wings, she grew wings."

* * *

In the stadium, the charged voice spoke into the microphone. "On the mound is the much-feared pitcher of the Puerto Rican team, Carlos Ortiz, while at the plate, hitting for the Dominicans, is Miguel Luí Paúl. And here it comes"—the Puerto Rican announcer said—"Blew it by him. Fast ball. Strike called! The crowd is going crazy."

Miguel Luí touched his chest and then stretched his arm out straight, pointing into the distance.

"That's an unspoken threat," the Dominican announcer said. "Miguel Luí, alias El Chu, has the most stratospheric average of the team." It was a tense moment, and the announcer barely had time to finish his sentence before he cried out, "Will you look at that! It's going, going, going, gone! That ball took wings and flew!"

As he ran, he could make out words in the exclamation of the human wave in the stands. He took his time, touching the bases, crossing himself and looking toward the sky. He acknowledged his fans with two fingers, touching them to his lips, to his chest, and then toward the crowd.

The Dominican flag waved from right to left, and tears could be seen from afar in the eyes of his countrymen, triumphal pride felt in every heart.

Moments before, in the dugout, his manager had heard him reciting, "The ball that grows wings is the one that goes astray." He repeated it maniacally to himself.

And then the loudspeakers announced, "Now batting for the Dominican team, Miguel Luí Paúl."

And the crowd screamed.

THE GLORY OF MAMPORAL

Andrés Eloy Blanco
(Venezuela)

This Venezuelan classic was first published in 1935. Andrés Eloy Blanco (1897–1955) was a poet, playwright, satirist, lawyer, and politician—a political prisoner because of his underground publishing activities in the 1920s, later congressman in the 1930s, president of the constitutional convention and then foreign minister in the 1940s, and finally a political exile in Mexico at the time of his death. All told, he published more than twenty books of poetry, plays, short stories, biography, and essays. Municipalities in three different Venezuelan states are named after him. So is the utility infielder Andrés Eloy Blanco (no relation), most recently of the Philadelphia Phillies and, in winter ball, the Navegantes de Magallanes.

"Come visit. Come and see a bit of my busy life in Mamporal. Please don't tell me that village life is tiresome while the rhythm of the city is exciting. That won't impress me at all." So I wrote yesterday in a letter to my friend Adriana, who is usually open to adventure. Then I added, "Mamporal is the capital of the world, if you will. For me, these days, it is the center of the solar system."

In the nation's capital they know nothing about the active, stormy, dizzying life of Mamporal. They have their cosmopolitan kaleidoscope, their automobiles, social divisions, and everything else that prevails in great urban centers. The result is that people are buried in new problems, so they forget the fever of the daily dramas, the hustle and bustle of domestic affairs, the small but sensational novelties and recurring conflicts that make village life as exhausting as that of any metropolis. To believe otherwise is to deny that the microscope reveals a universe as febrile as that of the telescope. Mamporal is the most lively city I know. Believe me, by knowing Mamporal I know all the world and taste all its delights.

Over the past thirty days truly sensational things have happened in this town. Many kinds of things, but each has affected the entire social body and impelled it to action. That does not happen in big cities: no totalization of an occurrence in the collective heart, no unanimity of emotion. But all of Mamporal is contained in every event.

The sensations of the past thirty days could be classified according to their intensity or other characteristics. But all of them, even the most transitory and banal, shake up the village—from house to house, all up and down the dusty street. Genuinely political events in Mamporalese life have nothing to do with national politics. Viewed from here, national politics seem a distant, nearly supernatural science. The high powers of the nation are of a weighty character far removed from local emotions. Our village, by contrast, is most aroused by commentary on our great local episodes. The Town Registrar, his Secretary, the Judge, and the Policeman make up the hamlet-as-nation. If a high official should happen to pay a visit, then the nation-as-hamlet comes into play.

The latest event of a political character, therefore, was a heated dispute between the Judge and the Secretary. The Secretary "went for his revolver," as we like to say. Men poured into the street, women summoned their husbands and children, and the sliding of door bolts echoed through the town. But the Registrar appeared and said the Judge was in the right. The Secretary walked slowly away, gathering admiring glances from the young ladies who watched him go by.

The social scandal, however, was the abuse of a girl on the Garambunda farm, revealed when her torn and bloody underwear was found. This was followed by my unexplained arrival. No one had explained why I'd come, or what I was searching for. For a week everyone eyed me with suspicion. Finally, I made a public statement that I was here to look into the case of assault. After six days of investigation, I arrested Francisco Sierra and sent him to the state capital. Now the people of Mamporal love me, and I've had the wit to declare that this place is my second home. Everyone tells me their secrets. I'm the consulting attorney here.

* * *

But the key event of the past month has been the encounter between the Mamporal Athletic Club and Nine Stars of Manatí. No one can remember comparable excitement since the days of the civil wars. And there is good reason for this, as anybody who knows Mamporal and Manatí will understand very well.

Mamporal and Manatí are neighbors, six leagues apart. But that is a deep and irreconcilable distance. Manatí is to Mamporal what Mr. Mussolini is to Mr. Modigliani, or Mr. Frías to Mr. Juan Ramos. Manatí is Guelph; Mamporal, Ghibelline. Manatí is Carthage; Mamporal, Rome. Manatí is the devil; Mamporal, the envoy of the Pope.

It is not uncommon to find such hatred between two neighboring towns. In fact, what's uncommon is not to find it. Borders make for hatred, proximity makes for resentment.

This, of course, depends on the relative importance of the towns. El Valle can't hate Caracas, because Caracas is so much more important. Arganda can hate Chinchón, but Chinchón can't hate Madrid. Mamporal and Manatí can hate each other, but neither one can hate Calabozo, which was the state capital once. Mamporal and Manatí hate each other like Dr. Paul's chauffeur and the Swiss ambassador's doorman, or the Swiss ambassador himself and the wife of Dr. Paul.

This enmity between Manatí and Mamporal is longstanding, but it has had its spontaneous peaks and crises. Often this is due to competition, to a given stimulus being exacerbated and poorly managed. At one time Manatí's local priest was a delightful old man, sweeter than a baby goat. Mamporal, however, was assigned a new, young priest—gallant, smelling of rosewater, a crooner of ballads and bits of opera. He could recite romantic poems from the past century in Mexico, he chewed on perfumed pills that sweetened his breath, and he led the mass with the air of a matador showing off his skills against bulls retired from the ring. Manatí wailed in protest until they had driven out their poor, old, peaceful priest and obtained a dandy who recited ditties from no less a land than Spain.

On another occasion the government decided to build a new highway through Manatí. In response, the Mamporalese refused to travel by land. They all went via the Apure River, prolonging their journeys by a good five days.

One day a player piano was unloaded in Manatí. The Manatíans sat down, row upon row of them, before the automatic device, and then each had a chance to make it play a song. The volume they coaxed out of the device seemed intended to be heard in Mamporal. Within a fortnight, Don Damián Robles of Mamporal had two player pianos in his house.

Things rose to such a pitch that on a certain unfortunate day, when a lightning bolt hit Mamporal and burned three houses to the ground, there was cheering in Manatí. "Mamporal is finished!" the Manatíans crowed.

But a few days later a serious problem arose, because Mamporal achieved a certain notoriety in the national press. The stories appeared in the papers of Calabozo and San Fernando and even in the two great dailies of the capital of the republic: "Catastrophe in Mamporal" . . . "In Aid of the Victims of Mamporal" . . . "Committee in Support of Mamporal." Manatí was alarmed, and soon four philanthropists offered their houses to be burned on the next available stormy night.

One day, the two towns each received a notice from the governor of the state. In lengthy and ponderous sentences, that official asserted a need for the more isolated villages to demonstrate self-reliance through their own deeds. "God helps those who help themselves," the document seemed to advise, and it instructed small communities not to expect all blessings to flow from state or national largesse. Rather, they were to stimulate their own efforts to achieve the modest conquests that Sanitation, Adornment, and Education allow only to the hardest-working communities. The circular concluded by recommending that local authorities and populations should create development councils "to serve as a permanent incentive, a wide-open valve for the initiation of dignifying activities" to meet "the urgent needs" of each locale.

Manatí proceeded to set up a council in accord with the recommendation. It was called the Council for Improvement of Manatí and was made up of merchants, ranchers, farmers, the local authorities, and, in sum, the cream of the town. Its admirable mission was described succinctly in a yellow flyer printed up for the purpose: "To oversee the continued progress of the town, provide for general needs, protect individual initiatives, and, in general, keep Manatí in the place of honor, the Privileged situation, that its hardworking sons have earned it."

The Mamporalese waited for Manatí to form its council, and, once aware of its program, they then launched their own. Theirs was called the Council of Progress of the Municipality of Mamporal. As a subtitle, their flyer declared, to wide approval, "Glory to the Queen of the Plains!" It went on: "The goals toward which the council is proceeding are the continual and incessantly growing greatness of our beloved Mamporal, the young sultana of the Plains. Thanks to our efforts, the tidal wave of Progress will forever wash over the smiling streets of our Privileged villa, which will emerge greater and greater in the Privileged situation brought on by its hardworking and heroic sons. Viva Mamporal!"

So far, no actual aspersions had been cast. But in a fiery speech on the day of the council's inauguration, the esteemed high school graduate Mirabal Villasmil allowed himself to say, "The Council of Progress of the Municipality of Mamporal shall make the witless snouts of our treacherous neighbors feel the eloquent blow of the back of our hand."

It also happened that, when a lady of Manatí was entering into the throes of labor, a call went out to Teobaldo, the male midwife of Mamporal—a repellent sort of fellow, his back half-twisted by a spinal ailment, with one eye turned toward Mamporal and the other toward Manatí. So Teobaldo set off in his lame gait and arrived to officiate at the birth of the new Manatían, and someone stuck a nose into the room and inquired, "What is it Teobaldo, a girl or a boy?"

Teobaldo, the midwife from Mamporal, displaying a strong newborn boy in his arms, answered most sweetly, "A girl. As always."

They wanted to kill him. But Teobaldo returned to Mamporal to recount over and over, to universal chuckles, the pasting he'd given "the fairies of Manatí."

But soon the confrontation between the two baseball teams became the dominating event. Mamporal won the first game, thirty-two runs to twenty, on twenty-seven hits. The return match, played in Manatí, went to the local team, the Nine Stars, thus tying the series. And the third and decisive game ended with no result. When the Mamporalese saw they were on the point of losing, all hell broke loose. The story goes like this:

In the eighth inning, with Manatí leading thirty-nine to twenty-three, a Mamporalese runner tried to steal second base. The *catcher* made a strong and perfect throw, grabbed by the second baseman who awaited the runner, blocking the base path while holding the ball. The Mamporal player stopped for an instant, then head-butted his antagonist in the chest. The fielder dropped the ball and fell to the ground, vomiting blood from his mouth and his nose. The runner dashed on to third and rounded toward home when the umpire stopped him.

"You're *ao*!"

"What do you mean *ao*? Call your grandmother *ao*!"

"But you . . ."

"One moment," the Mamporalese captain intervened. "What's going on here?"

"The gentleman is *ao*."

"*Ao*? The fielder interfered with his running."

"No sir. Your runner head-butted him."

"No more than he deserved."

A group formed around them, compact and threatening. The Manatíans gathered, too, gripping their bats. The umpire, unintimidated, shouted, "Forfeit! I declare the game a forfeit, in favor of the Nine Stars!"

"The Nine Stars? A thousand stars are what you're going to see," and they clobbered him with a swing of the bat that left him flat on his back, blood spurting even from his ears.

As havoc threatened, the Registrar intervened. He represented the national authority. Tempers cooled.

"Now, friends," he said. "The man on second is not *ao,* because the other one got in his way. But he is being turned over to the police. As for the game, it's called on account of rain. We'll decide the championship another day."

The only thing raining was the harsh rays of the sun. The Nine Stars sauntered off. The high school graduate Mirabal Villasmil declared, "If Mamporal loses, what you just saw is only the beginning."

* * *

The next piece of news fell on Mamporal like a bomb. The consternation was unprecedented. On April 19 a bust of the national hero Colonel Julio Rondón was slated to be unveiled in the town square of Manatí. Rondón, born in Manatí, was the pride of the armies of the plains.

Desolation was widespread, and not without reason. A catastrophe had befallen Mamporal, leaving it humiliated overnight—depopulated, destroyed, a thousand leagues beneath its hated rival. The reason was clear. Manatí would have its town square and its bust, because Manatí had its hero. Mamporal had no hero, no glory, nothing at all.

Well, Mamporal did have its town square, but up till then no one had ever thought of using it for anything but market day, or tying up burros, or the solitary parading of the occasional wandering nighttime cow. At most, it might be possible to consider building a monument to Bolívar or Páez, but as far as any local "glory," any glory of its own, any glory as anyone's place of birth, there was simply nothing to be done.

* * *

The Council of Progress of the Municipality of Mamporal was in session. Considering the gravity of the situation, member Francisco de Paula Vera suggested that "by any means necessary, the erection of the unfortunate bust of Julio

Rondón must be prevented." The Registrar, however, protested in the name of individual freedom.

"Whose fault is it that you don't have anyone to honor?" he asked. "In Carora where I'm from, we have Pedro León Torres."

The high school graduate Mirabal Villasmil, secretary of the council, made a proposal. It was seconded by Don Antonio Karama, a Syrian, owner of the tiny inn. "The glory of having given birth to Colonel Julio Rondón, illustrious Father of our Independence, should be challenged, since there are indications that he was born in Calabozo and not in Manatí."

Teobaldo the midwife rejected that proposition.

"No, sir, Julio Rondón was born in Manatí. Even the alley cats know that. And his baptismal certificate is there."

Felipe Rauta tentatively put in a word. "What if we could show that Julio Rondón was really a jerk. . . ."

"Never!" the Registrar retorted. "That would be an action against one of the glories of our nation."

"Then there's nothing more to talk about. What else is there to do?"

"There is one thing," old Teobaldo suggested slyly.

"One thing? And what's that?"

"Well . . . a bust."

"Another bust? Of whom?"

"I don't know. In my house I've got big bronze one. It's been there a long time."

"But who is it?"

"I don't know. Maybe Rojas Paúl, from Andueza . . . I don't know. Maybe Vargas."

"But who does it look like?"

"Nobody. That much I can say for sure. It's been sitting for twenty years in a corner of my wife's room. I don't know how it ended up there. But what I can say for sure is that it doesn't look like anyone."

"Then," the high-school graduate Mirabal Villasmil exclaimed, "we're saved! *Viva* Mamporal! *Viva* Mamporal! *Viva* Mamporal!"

Teobaldo echoed, "*Viva* Mamporal!"

That last *Viva!*, in the mouth of the male midwife, sound like a birth, the birth of a hero.

* * *

On April 19, at the same time as the launching of fireworks in Manatí to welcome the first bronze effigy of Colonel Julio Rondón, the brave combatant from the plains, in the clean and sundrenched town square of Mamporal the Registrar pulled away a white sheet to unveil the bronze bust of a severe looking man wrapped in an equally severe civilian cloak. Its pedestal held a simple and noble inscription:

Mamporal is grateful to its benefactor.

A NOTORIOUS HOME RUN

Cezanne Cardona Morales
(Puerto Rico)

Born in 1982, Cezanne Cardona Morales is a novelist, short story writer, professor, and columnist. In 2009 he won one of Puerto Rico's most prestigious literary awards, the Short Story Prize of the newspaper El Nuevo Día. *In 2010 he published his first novel,* La velocidad de lo perdido *(Editorial Terranova, Barcelona). In 2011 he was included in* El ojo del huracán, *the new anthology of Puerto Rican short story writers (Grupo Editorial Norma).*

I owe center fielder Reba Kigali's story to the intersection of a genocide and a grand slam. Though I remember the first time I saw Reba's name, in a list of prospects during the big league strike of 1994, it wasn't till he hit the homer in the '96 World Series—a homer that almost cost us the championship—that I understood the stain it bore.

I can still hear the ironic laughs that were the automatic reaction of all three of us on base when Reba Kigali stepped up to the plate. I was on first, because my single to left had just moved the other runners over. That was enough to bring the crowd to life, even as they were beginning to file out in the face of imminent defeat. It was the bottom of the ninth, the Atlanta Braves had seven runs, and we, the Yankees, only four. Though there were no outs, I doubted we still had the makings of a last-minute miracle in the tank. The Braves' manager called time and walked out to visit his star hurler, Greg Maddux, on the mound. His glove in front of his face to prevent anyone from reading his lips, Greg talked with the manager. Neither of them looked nervous. Maybe they were reciting the world's best poems. Probably the manager was offering the usual advice. Either way, Greg knew he wasn't about to be pulled. Most likely the advice was just what he expected: fast ball, then something filthy for the batter to flail at, then a curve and Kigali would be out of there. It's hard to fault them. Throughout the '95 season, Reba Kigali had been the best hitter on the team, but this year he'd been in such a slump that the rumor mill said nobody wanted to pick up his contract, not even the Cubs, worst team in either league, even worse than the Pirates in their dog days. Given his constant bouts of depression, Reba was about to be consigned to Double-A, the cemetery of ballplayers and the back door to paradise for those who still believed in dreams.

Early in '95, though, it was obvious why he'd been hired. Reba was an outstanding outfielder, and he soon hit his way into the starting lineup with an average of .375. There was just one thing that struck everyone as strange, as well as provoking the deep-seated racism to which we blacks are not immune. Reba always cried when he hit a home run. He cried the way only brave men who know how to cry can do. I don't know whether this was involuntary or it was intended to make us forget the terrible story that was always told about him. All I can say is that his repeated action seemed like a kind of unction, a stylized expression of pain, or even a device to provoke his notable and imminent disappearance.

Reba had reached the big leagues amid glorious comparisons to Josh Gibson, the "black Babe Ruth" of the Negro leagues in the 1940s. But Reba seemed to be pursuing Josh's psychotic side, beset as he was by some sort of attacks of rage or madness, like what happened to Gibson when he was playing in the Puerto Rican winter league of 1945 and was arrested for stumbling drunk and naked through Old San Juan in search of the airport. Reba had also missed his flight, apparently forever. The last time anyone calculated his career numbers, his batting average stood at .190, and he looked clumsy at best in center field. No kids flocked to the exit gate for him to sign cards, balls, gloves, or the breasts of their single mothers who came with them, one of the best perks of the line of work we're in. I seem to remember being present when Kigali asked a photographer to surrender the film of him crying over one of his last home runs, one of the weakest and flimsiest of his career. How could anyone suddenly lose the genius for the game the way he did? There are plenty of theories. Some of them are even sensible: Genius is nothing but the residue of luck.

Back then I thought I knew what was going on—or had a good guess, at least. It wasn't that Kigali wanted to escape his career, but that he wanted to escape himself, and baseball provided the exit. Wasn't that only fair, given the crime he had supposedly committed? The few times I heard him speak, he was talking about players who had made costly mistakes in crucial games. He told me about all the times Ted Williams struck out in the late innings instead of saving the game. His nerves got the best of him, Reba said. It felt like self-justification, but there was more to it than that. He described those games in an uncanny way, as if he'd been there himself, though that was impossible, because those miscues took place before we were even spermatozoa running our first marathons.

Of all the mistakes he narrated, the one he most like to tell involved not just one standout player, but two—Mickey Mantle and Joe DiMaggio, like two astronomical bodies crashing in a dark, starlit sky. It happened during Mantle's rookie year, 1951. In the fifth inning of the second game of the World Series, he came charging out of right field to capture a blast by Willie Mays. But the great DiMaggio, who was in center, went after it too. It was a duel, a race to end all races, Mantle and DiMaggio like Achilles and Hector, each running after an out that wouldn't, in fact, change the result of the game or the series. Neither one called for the ball. At last minute, DiMaggio did call it. Mantle, just before crashing into DiMaggio, who knew he was right there, stopped and tore the ligaments in his knee. Mick wanted to shine, to make an impression as a rookie, and indeed he owed some of his immortality to that mistake, that devastating excess of rookie ego that wanted to outshine a giant like DiMaggio. The cry of pain and then the bad knee that followed him the rest of his career gave Mantle the best years of his life, a sour victory of pain and glory. Anything he did wrong, it was the fault of his damn knees; anything he did right, you had to marvel about how someone with busted ligaments could play so well. It's all about finding the lesion, the wound, the failure, the death in life that will save us from a life that's worse.

When the Braves' manager left the mound and we saw that Maddux was indeed staying in the game, we knew it was over. I remember glancing at the first baseman and him telling me not to take much of a lead, because the bases were loaded and I'd soon have to come back in humiliation, because Kigali was a sure out. It wanted to tell him the opposite, just like I always do, but I decided to leave him to the noisy silence of his conscience. Of all sports, baseball accepts failure most easily. We've all struck out, we've all been hit by a ball that has sent us to first base or to nowhere, we've all swung at a curve that avoids our bat, we've all let the best pitch go by, the pitch to hit, the one that turns out to be right over the plate, fooling us till our last sudden sigh. Maybe it was this pulse of failure that made me fall in love with baseball as a kid, maybe that's why I was able to find more imaginary fathers in the game. After a while you realize that you can only play baseball if you know how to embrace your own anger, how to be as big as your own nonexistence. And, besides that, it's the only sport that lets you adjust the position of your cock and balls in front of thousands of people, as naturally as you might adjust your glove or you might toss off an insult at Homer or at God.

I came out of my stupor to listen to the pointless silence that precedes the pitcher winding up. Straight down the middle, a swing, a faint, futile breeze, and back I went to first base. I swore at the African—the Rwandese, as he clarified for me once from his full height of six feet six. Reba was broad-shouldered—he looked like he'd been a boxer before taking up baseball—and in his well-sculpted muscles there was a music of hunger and poverty, among the best sources of muscle in the world.

The first baseman told me what I'd already heard about Reba, but I hadn't confirmed that it was true, and I don't know whether I ever will. In Rwanda, he claimed, Reba's father was a famous announcer and radio station owner who broadcast the play-by-play of baseball games gone by, but he was also an activist for the Hutu people and never lost a chance to insult their enemies, the Tutsi, who had, thanks to the Belgians, enslaved the Hutu for years. When the time of Hutu vengeance came, after several unsuccessful revolutions, Reba had no option but to join the Interahamwe, which, I read recently, meant simply enough, "Let us hit together."

"Look at him," the first baseman said, showing off what he'd recently learned. "Can't you see him, machete in hand? Don't you see how he's looking at his bat? Eight hundred thousand dead in a hundred days. Those Hutu were more effective than the Nazi bastards or the Communist clowns. A model genocide. You'd better believe it, and don't go pitying him because he happens to be on your team. That fucking

African is guilty of genocide. And don't tell me there isn't any proof."

I watched Reba stand up straight, inches away from home plate, where he'd never stand again. I crept a little bit away from the bag. Kigali banged his bat against his spikes to loosen the dirt that had been stuck there, then spat on the ground. I don't know why we do this, but we do it better than anyone. I spat, too, like someone automatically copying a yawn. Reba regarded his bat with the confidence of a samurai admiring the perfection of his sword. The pitcher decided not to spit on the ball, given the tighter enforcement of that prohibition since the '70s, and instead filled his hand with saliva, which was almost the same thing. (Spit on a baseball is like the vaseline on a boxer's face.) He straightened his cap, studied the catcher's sign, said yes like a teenager on his first visit to the bordello, bent his knees, gave a look over to first, and threw a curve that ended up in the dirt underneath a hollow sound. Strike two. I swore at Reba again.

"A scout who'd had his eyes on Reba for years took advantage of the conflict in Rwanda to get him out of there at the cheapest price. Did the scout know this fucking African was a killer?" the first baseman asked. "They say that when the Hutu soldiers got to the school where Reba worked, they asked him, since he was a ranking Hutu, to tell who were Tutsi. Reba didn't know how to answer, so they put a machete in his hand and made him choose, out of all his pupils, which ones he thought they were." I listened to the first baseman and continued edging off the bag until a glance from the pitcher made me think he was going to try a pickoff throw. But Greg Maddux threw another pitch and Reba grazed the ball by mistake. I say by mistake because he didn't make any attempt to run or even to see where the ball had landed. The umpire pulled another one out of his impossible pockets and handed it to the catcher. I went back to first.

With two strikes on Reba, I tried to find a little calm. I

thought about my mother, who was a big baseball fan and had a boyfriend who taught me to love the game when I was still a kid who knew he could win every impossible war and the greatest invisible championships. My mother wanted me to fall in love with reading, too, because she was a professor of humanities in several universities back home in our country. I must have been seven or eight when I realized she'd gotten tired of looking for heroes. I found an old baseball card covered with kisses, crimson imprints from what seemed like centuries ago. She used baseball to get me started reading. For years she talked to me about Homer and the sports of the Achaeans and Trojans. My mother had a theory: in baseball, as in Greek literature, a mistake could add dignity. Much later, just before she died, I would pray for a losing game, even make a few errors toward that end, just to conjure a call from her. I'd lift the receiver and after an affectionate greeting and tender silence, my mother would read me passages from the Iliad where the gods look at mortals with understanding and disdain, because they know better than anyone how war is a game that serves to provoke the best errors of all. Often she told me about the wrath of Achilles, about hubris—as my mother said, with her intellectual tone—as if that were his best error, his style of winning immortality. It was the same in baseball: heroes make mistakes, she said, but what matters is their style. Strike out, fail to catch a ball, dive for it in vain—that's like the moment when Zeus transforms himself into a swan, into a rain shower, to make love to the woman he fancies and provoke the anger of another god.

But Reba, it seemed, had no intention of redeeming his glorious errors. Now we had to trust to luck. Not any old luck but the kind that's left after intelligence is of no more use. All the better—what we had left was the kind of faith you have in the wind, the heat, the cold. Or in lightness when there's nothing to do but float.

I expected Maddux's next pitch to be out of the zone.

That was the best way to ring someone up after two strikes. A bad pitch that looked good ought to drive the hitter to a desperation swing, with high chances of a foul, a pop-up, or a strikeout, the way Achilles would grow impatient in his wrath. I had heard the story the first baseman told me, but in a different version. Kigali couldn't choose any of his pupils, so he chose them all. But he asked the Hutu soldiers, in honor of his father, to let the children play the last game of their lives. The last one. Kigali called them all together in the yard and almost forced them to take the field. He put the smallest in the outfield—center, right, and left—and whispered something in their ears. The kids laid out the bases, shards of zinc painted white that threatened to inflict tetanus on the first runner to slide. The kids found the only bat they had, and they didn't look at the dry mud of the field, so they could imagine the impossible green of a true baseball field. In this game all his pupils would play against him. The soldiers sat in the truck that had brought them, impassively smoking their cigarettes. Reba pointed his bat toward the woods on the edge of the field like Kevin Costner in *Field of Dreams*, pointing to the cornfield, the paradise of washed-up baseball men. But the first baseman insisted that my version was false, that the notion of Kigali placing his pupils in the field so that on his first hit they'd take off and hide in the woods was a terrible lie. "The next out you're going to see," he told me, "will be made by a killer who put them in the field maliciously so he could see his vengeance come true: his first home run was going to be greeted by the applause of machetes and bullets."

Kigali watched the pitch approach, a bit low and outside, a perfect home run ball, but he didn't swing. Our Caribbean style of turning bad pitches into homers had not found any echo in him. I'm sure that, before the umpire signaled it had been off the plate, Kigali wanted it to be the strike that would end his career. But that's not how it went. What none of us expected was that Kigali would slug the next pitch straight to center and out of the park. The dull sound of the bat still echoes in my memory, a noise like that of clinking two mugs full of beer, the way I never did with Reba, barhopping in search of women. That swing unleashed an orgy of happiness in the stadium, a roar it would be sacrilege to call jubilation. What no one yet knew was that we were still on the point of losing the championship, but now due to a notorious home run. My only thoughts were about crossing the plate, the photos in *Sports Illustrated*, the glorious hugs and slaps of victory in counterpoint to the dying dreams of the other team.

But when I reached the plate, I saw that Kigali was still rounding second, looking sluggish, as if we were playing on Jupiter and forced into slow motion by the massive gravity there. Was he overcome with emotion? Was it a heart attack, or would he fall to the ground like Josh Gibson, suffering from a brain tumor he had no inkling of? Could he have hit a home run in that game in front of the Hutu soldiers? Whatever my guess, I couldn't have imagined what happened next. I ran toward third to urge him on. But he'd already sat down, like a child chastised by a parent, his head between his legs and rocking from side to side. Had he bet against his own team? When I got close to him, I didn't know what to think. Underneath my laughter what I felt was pity. There was no god accompanying that desolate condition, so I knew he wasn't praying. He was sitting and crying like I'd never seen before, sitting in the dirt of the base path a few inches from third, still far from home. Was he saying, *It was all I could do, I told them to run as fast as they could, I yelled for them to run, to get into the woods*? The umpire declared that if Reba didn't touch home plate, the game would be tied and go into extra innings. Everyone, me among them, was urging him to get moving, but Kigali just shook his head. He didn't want to move. Whoever heard of a ballplayer refusing to run the bases after his own home run? Nobody in the world has that kind of freedom. I knew that if I laid even a finger on Reba the umpire would call one of us out for interference and that would be that. But when I tried yelling at him again, Reba got up and hit me with a right cross that split my lip. *I'm no Hutu,* I said—or thought—*and no Tutsi either, friend. All I want is to win the Series.*

Everyone fell silent, the umpires too. Kigali made threatening gestures to anyone who came near him. He was crying to beat the band, and cursing, screaming insults, possessed by gods or saints unknown. While I was recovering from his punch, I made out a strange phrase that I recognized from a story I had read in junior high, a story I hadn't been able to make sense of at all. "I would prefer not to." Could anyone refuse to circle the bases after a four-bagger? Could Kigali refuse to choose? Was it better to die? Was it worse to be the witness who prevented anyone from forgetting what happened? I remembered an article I read about a schoolmaster in the Rwandan capital who survived a massacre, and when the conflict was over he gathered all the bodies he found on his route home and put them in his living room, so no one could claim that the genocide never occurred. The reporter wrote that you had to wear a mask to go in there, because of the stench, and you had to carry a handful of lime to aid in the decomposition, as if the visitors to that improvised museum were pitchers or gymnasts, weightlifters or sluggers, any athletes who have to dust their hands for a grip that helps them overcome gravity, inertia, or wind.

The umpire and the manager went over to him, but Kigali threw dirt in their eyes and then tossed his helmet at them. We'd moved from baseball to boxing to hardcore wrestling and then to—literature? What could this be but literature in action, as my mother used to say in her effort to help me understand the times when reason and logic no long apply, but metaphors come into play: the moments in life when tragedy and comedy merge to explain pointlessness. I thought that maybe if I pulled off one of Reba's shoes and carried it to the plate, then the run would score and we'd win the Series after all, but the umpire rejected my crazy idea without so much as a reason for his call. And how was I going to get the shoe off a giant a foot taller than me?

That was when, in spite of the umps yelling at us, we pickup up Kigali and carried him home against his will. Almost the whole team piled in, hoisting him to our shoulders and running like we were carrying a wounded soldier on the point of being incinerated by our own napalm. Then we put him down on the plate. In all the history of baseball I've never known anyone who had the privilege or notoriety of touching the plate against his will. Later on we'd invent excuses: Kigali had hurt his knee and couldn't walk, he'd had a panic attack, whatever. Meanwhile, the homer could not be denied. As soon as we stopped running he resumed cursing and insulting us from the bottom of his heart, flailing out with every part of his body, and then shouting names—the names of his pupils, so that they'd run. There were fourteen or fifteen names, and Kigali never knew how many got away. Was there any point in knowing that now? How many perverted men have committed acts of justice? How many just men have committed perverse acts?

A nurse came out to sedate him with a dose of Demerol so he could be carried off the field in a stretcher. Before the paramedics took him away, Reba looked at me asking for my pardon. I thought that was just for having split my lip, but then I understood it went way beyond that. Was it absolution that Kigali was after? Yes, but the kind for someone who couldn't do any more, forgiveness without understanding, details, or recrimination, an absolution very close to forgetting, like the pitch we're inclined to let go by for fear of success and failure. Was it better to die and not be a witness, or to survive so as to tell, to save whatever still seemed salvageable by then? I remembered what Reba had said about Mantle and DiMaggio running after the fly ball. The injury Mantle needed for his career, the injury that would bring him immortality. Had Reba achieved the injury we all seek for the time when everything turns out wrong? Did such a thing exist? I didn't say a word. I stood there looking at him until they carried him away, just before the sounds of celebration invaded that companionable silence. I smiled at him, but without compassion. The crowd began to cheer, though still afraid that Kigali might be a traitor who had bet against his team, or other such theories that didn't make much sense. Self-assured or not, the applause came, and Kigali raised his hand from the stretcher in a gesture of farewell. He said goodbye to his career and to his pupils whom he had managed to save or not. He said goodbye to his career with a notorious home run that almost cost us the championship.

THE PITCHER

Marcial Gala
(Cuba)

Marcial Gala was born in Havana in 1963 and now lives in the city of Cienfuegos. He is the author of the novels Sentada en su verde limón (2004), La catedral de los negros (2012), and Monasterio (2013), published in Cuba and Spain, as well as five books of stories and two of poetry. La catedral de los negros won both of Cuba's most important national awards, Premio Carpentier and Premio de la Crítica. His stories have been anthologized in Cuba, Puerto Rico, and Argentina. Before beginning his literary career, he studied both psychiatric ergotherapy and architecture.

Sixty feet away from me, the catcher calls for a strike. The players are ready. I feel the weight of the whole stadium on my shoulders. The batter grips the bat, fiercely seeking eye contact, and now he's waiting, too. He's a good hitter. I can sense his nose more than I can see it—like a bloodhound's nose, the nostrils dilating in expectation of my delivery. The delivery that I'm not going to begin. I could turn toward first and throw the ball over there, toward the carefree runner who thinks the game is only a game. Maybe he's right, since all he has to do is run to second, oblivious of anything else, and slide in quickly, ahead of the ball. I'm the one who throws the ball, and as I said, the crowd is on my shoulders. I don't know how long I can hold out. The batter waits, waving his bat in a circle, watching me. This isn't the first time we've faced each other. It's never the first time.

"*Pónchalo*! Strike him out!" the fans scream, their minds fixed on the game, incapable of understanding me. I can't make them out; to me they're just a maddening swath of color. And what am I to them? Less than that. To them I'm something simple, just an arm, a catapult ready to unload, that's what it all comes down to, they think. In the radio and television booths the announcers must be saying, "The *pitcher* is taking his time." That tautological sentence defines me as the proverbial tortoise, dragging out the game, while in other multiple and infinitesimal worlds, brief lives begin and end. A drop of sweat slides along the dark skin of my hand until it reaches the leather of the ball. In that drop, I can see myself. If I looked at it, I could understand this game, this stadium, and this crowd. If I could understand the drop of sweat, but I can't, no way. The sweat falls into the dirt. Now my teammates are getting nervous. "Nothing to worry about, go for it!" one of them yells. "No batter, no batter," another one chips in. The batter is a cornered animal, and so am I. If only they knew I'm not going to throw, I'm going to wait until the afternoon ends or someone calls the game. The umpires won't do it. They don't understand any better than me. The fans could do it, but the fans are screaming, they want me to throw this leather sphere in the shortest possible arc into the glove of the man crouching behind *home*.

"A strike!" the multitude demands, while the runner on first advances slowly, carefully, like a hungry deer approaching a river in spite of sensing the leopard nearby. He abandons the security of the base, keeping an eye on my back; I know that

that's what he's doing even though I can't see him. If I turned, it would be easy to trap him and get the third out. But wouldn't that just prolong my agony? Sooner or later, wouldn't another inning begin, another game with its terrible, heavy weight? I'm the leopard, but I'm the tortoise, too. This is no game; I've learned enough to know that. The game starts when the lights go off, when the losers and the winners and the delirious fans go home. Then we play at being cooks, mechanics, doctors, politicians, slackers, husbands, mothers, and children. Then the game seems to have stopped, but then the next one starts the endless nightmare all over. What would it be like to play at being dead, I wonder, and I know that's a metaphor, because death is surely a surprise, and that's why I'm so afraid to throw the ball. What would I be without this round, white certainty in my hands? Now I'm the hunter, the leopard, the pitcher, but then, when my defenseless eyes watch the umpire's hands, watch his face chiseled in stone, watch his fallible mouth and await his judgment? Then, in those seconds, the terrible sensation of being just a ghost under my uniform will come over me, a specter imagined by the devious crowd, and what can I do then . . . ?

Now the manager of our team is worried, too. I see him walking from one end of the *dogao* to the other, watching me. He's worried about more than the delay, I can tell; it's as if he knew I'd decided not to pitch anymore. He has an uncanny ability to guess what I'm thinking, but that's encouraging, it shows that all is not lost, that through my agony and immobility I can communicate something, at least. It's not that I think I'm better than anyone. If I don't pitch, that won't disturb the universe, I know. They'll just bring in another pitcher, and some fans, not so many, will leave the stadium, turn off the TV, say the game is lost without me, say that not even baseball is like it used to be. But can the game be lost? That's such a well-worn word, lost. The only ones lost are us, insignificant pebbles rolling along and thinking we're immortal. I won't be the pitcher anymore, that's all. I won't have that dark responsibility on my shoulders. All I have to do is close my eyes, and the delirious crowd, the anguished multitude demanding something unknown and unacceptable to me, will disappear. All I have to do is close my eyes, cover my ears, maybe, and then what will be left of the game, or of us? Will I have the courage to do that, to escape from their expectations? Can I cease to be the pitcher just because I say so? Then, without that identity, what will I be? Nothing, or almost nothing. I'll walk off slowly, very slowly, toward the showers underneath the stands, while the absurd mass of spectators follows me with their eyes and screams, "Yellow!" Yellow means coward. Will I have the courage to confront my defeat? Can I see myself as a coward, I, who so often have beaten the best our opponents have to offer? I can picture the headlines in tomorrow's papers: *Pitcher self-destructs. Pitcher blows up, unable to hold opponents in check*. But that explosion is not real. It's just that I, the pitcher, am in deadly pain.

Now the umpire, that crow in human form, despairs. I can almost see the slight rictus of bitterness in his mouth, only partly hidden by the leather and iron of his mask. His eyes lock onto the ball, more than onto me. He still expects that one second or another, like a harlequin puppet, I'll lift my right leg, raise it almost to my chest, and then bring my left arm back and bring it forward as fast as I can in a convoluted motion, fingers gripping the sphere and then letting it go. Will it be a ball or a strike? Who can say? Time passes, that's all we know. Ten years I've devoted to the rude pastime of throwing a simple leather sphere into a padded leather glove. I confess it, I've aged, and my body that looks so robust has been eaten away by secret ills. Last night, in the bus on the way to the hotel, I fell asleep and dreamed of a beautiful morning in a stadium where I was the batter and the pitcher was You who are listening to me. How could I guess what pitch You were going to throw? Which of Your orbs, You who are master of so many worlds, was destined for me? Could I expect benevolence? Could I expect forgiveness for my absolute inability to hit off of such as You? But I had a modicum of confidence, because if Jacob wrestled with You, why couldn't I? So I gripped the bat even though You are so big and I am the feeblest of dwarfs. I almost went blind gazing on Your splendor so as to guess the moment when You would deign to pitch to me. I was sure the umpire was on Your side, the fans too, and all the players in the world and all those who aren't players as well, all of them one way or another were You, and I could even feel the part of You that dwells in me. Me alone against You, trembling, but with a tiny, remote, almost nonexistent shard of hope. I thought You could understand the hunger in my heart. But You never threw the pitch, and we stood there for an eternity, face to face, while the umpire prepared for his inevitable cry of "Out!" Now here I am, I'm the pitcher, and the players and fans are waiting for me, but I'm never going to throw. Do You know that? I'm going to let the batter agonize in wait. I want to believe that this batter is You. If so, how will the crowd react when they see a player with eyes so tender making his way to the batter's box with the innocence of a lamb? The multitude will hush when they see You, Lord, or their shouts will grow even more delirious, or maybe they will sense at last that this is not a game. I imagine that slender player choosing a bat the way he might choose a chalice. I imagine him holding it clumsily, the wrong end in his grip, smiling at the crowd as they cry "Yellow!" Smiling at me, Your enemy, and against my will I'm going to hit You in the head with a projectile thrown at a speed never before seen. I know this, and I know Your son will die, but no, Lord, forgive me, I am Your son, now I understand, You created this stadium around me so that I can convince this restive multitude that is so intent on the game and expecting so much of me. But what can I say to them or what can I do, if You created me able to throw a ball and nothing more? Shall I raise my arms and plead for silence so I can present Your message to them? But what is Your message, Lord, what?

"Strike!" the umpire cried.

AUT AT THIRD

Vicente Leñero
(Mexico)

Vicente Leñero was born in Guadalajara in 1933 and died in Mexico City in 2011. Winner of Mexico's National Arts and Sciences Prize in 2001, he was a journalist, dramatist, screenwriter, novelist, and editor. He was among the founders of the magazine Proceso. *His eighteen screenplays include* El crimen del Padre Amaro, *nominated for the Oscar for Best Foreign Film in 2003. He was the coeditor, with Gerardo de la Torre, of* Pisa y corre *(Tagging Up), the 2005 pioneer anthology of Mexican baseball literature. Besides the play that follows, he wrote another one-act theater piece,* El fílder de destino *(Fielder of Destiny), in which a shortstop exiled to right field is addressed by the voices of a pair of poets as he pounds his glove and awaits the next fly ball.*

Characters:

CHATO MÉNDEZ

MANAGER

CARMEN

THIRD BASEMAN

ÁMPAYA [Hereafter the stage directions will say *umpire* for ease of reading.]

RUNNER (CHATO's stunt double)

Staging:

Three different areas can be seen.

- The area around third base on the ball field of a professional-league stadium. As if to isolate this area from the rest of the field, the lighting falls exclusively on the base, the chalk line dividing fair and foul territory, and the trodden dirt around the base, in which the third baseman moves. Home plate, which is invisible, would lie in the audience.
- The corner of the players' clubhouse within the stadium. A bench with no back, and lockers.
- The corner of an apartment.

The third base umpire, standing in foul territory, waits for the next play. We hear the sound of bat hitting ball. The motions of the third baseman and the umpire convey that the ball has landed safely in left center field, which cannot be seen. Seconds go by. The third baseman moves to cover the base. A base runner from the opposing team (who had been on first at the outset of the play) appears, running toward third. The baseman awaits the throw. The runner slides. The throw comes in from center field, a lightning throw, fast and strong, into the fielder's glove. He lowers his glove to tag the sliding runner. It's a close play. The umpire, with an emphatic gesture, unhesitatingly signals an out. The runner, CHATO MÉNDEZ, *jumps up furiously.*

CHATO. He didn't tag me! (*Pause.*) I slid in first, dammit. He didn't touch me! (*The umpire is impassive while* CHATO *angrily confronts him.*) I was *seif*, dammit! *Seif*! Are you blind? He didn't tag me! . . . What did they do, ump, bribe you? (*The umpire gives* CHATO *a challenging look.*) You crooked sonofa—. (*He moves away, still furious.*) It was clear as day. (*Mumbles to himself.*) Motherfuckers. (*Pause.*) *Aut*! That was no *aut*! He's blind as a bat.

The umpire moves away from CHATO *and ignores his outburst. Convinced he won't change the call, but still muttering protests,* CHATO *begins moving away from the base, his uniform stained with dirt from his slide. The lighting fades until the area disappears.* CHATO *proceeds toward the clubhouse bench. He flings his cap angrily into the distance and sits down. The* MANAGER *appears, an older man wearing the same uniform as* CHATO. *He's very angry too. During the manager's speeches,* CHATO *takes off his uniform and his spikes.*

MANAGER. I don't believe it. I really don't believe it! . . . Who the hell told you to go to third? . . . With two *auts*! . . . You were the tying run. You needed to hold up at second. And what did you do?

CHATO. I was *seif*.

MANAGER. *Seif* my ass. They had you cold. . . . Didn't you look at the coach? Did the coach send you? . . . Why can't you ever pay attention to me? What's the third base coach there for? If he sends you, you go. If not, you stay put. . . . And he held his hands up, I saw him, to tell you to hold at second. . . . But no, you always have to be the hero. All of you.

CHATO. I was *seif*.

MANAGER. Sure you were! . . . The same old thing. Don't I know it. Every time. You do something stupid, like you were playing all by yourselves, and then it's the umpire's fault. (*Mimicking.*) I was *seif*. . . . Shit! What a sorry excuse. Why do I break my ass teaching you how to play this fucking game? It's useless. . . . And you above all,

Chato. Making bonehead running plays on your own say-so like the coach is just painted there and I'm an idiot. . . . I don't know what to do with you, I really don't. (*While he speaks, the third base area lights up again, but this time dimly, like a ghost scene. The earlier action on the field repeats. The sound of ball hitting bat, a sound of excitement from the crowd, and the third baseman going to cover the base. A runner—*CHATO*'s double—charges toward the base at full speed. He slides and is tagged out. The umpire makes the call. The light goes out. The* MANAGER, *without interruption, continues speaking.*) You have to remember the score, how many times do I have to tell you! If we've got two *auts* and we're in the ninth in a tie game, who the hell tries to take an extra base? What good is one fucking base? . . . The Mouse's hit was short, you saw it, shallow in the outfield, almost a Texas Leaguer. On a hit like that you stop at second, you don't even need the coach. Take it easy, stop at second, let Martínez knock you in. . . . Martínez is a lefty, did you even think about that? He was going to pull the ball. For sure. He's hitting .302 and that pitcher couldn't find the plate. It was obvious. And his *slaider* wasn't breaking. (*Pause.*) The thing is, you never stop to think, Chato, and this game is played with your brain, not your balls. That's what you never understand. You keep thinking like a country boy—if there's a hit, run like a spooked mule. Very nice. And why? To show off? Now you see what that gets you, how the fuck do you look now?

CHATO. I was *seif*.

MANAGER. How can you say that, Chato? My God, even your own mother wouldn't have called you *seif*. As soon as you rounded second, I said, "This guy is dead." As a doornail. . . . The worst of it is, you knew what this game meant. What we needed was to get into extra innings. Then we'd have had it wrapped up. They would've needed a new pitcher, and the only arm they had left was that jerk Maldonado, who couldn't get three straight *auts* even against Puebla. . . . We were in the middle of a rally, Chato. The tying run. Your run. You were it. Everything depended on you. . . . And that's no good. It's no good. You can't do whatever you want. Run the bases on your slightest hunch. What am I supposed to . . . You can't do this to your team. Or to your manager, either.

CHATO. I took a chance because I thought I'd make it. . . . And I did make it. I was *seif*.

MANAGER. If you say that again, you bastard, I'll really fuck you up. So shut it. (*A long silence.* CHATO *has finished undressing, he's sitting on the bench in his shorts. Thinking. The* MANAGER *stays where he's been standing, shaking his head until he begins speaking again. Lights come up on the third base area again, diffuse and ghostly. The action of the third baseman tagging* CHATO *repeats. In the middle of the play, the* MANAGER *resumes speaking.*) Now we're a whisker away from being eliminated. Screwed. . . . We'd need to sweep the Tecolotes, and for Puebla to beat the Tigers at least once. But that's tough. The Tecolotes are on a roll. They've won six in a row, three of them shutouts. Two series sweeps. And that lefty, Esparza, is somebody to worry about. You knew that better than anybody, right? Didn't he whiff you twice the last time? Or was it three times? However it was, he killed us that game, and with fastballs, nothing but fastballs, about a hundred twenty miles an hour. . . . Probably it'll be him in the first game, that's who Carmona will put on the mound—if we're not already packing our bags, that is. (*Pause.*) I'm not saying we can't beat them, sure we can beat them, we've got the best lineup in the league, look at the numbers, but we need to really want it. And not only that, but everybody's got to do his job. Do his job, and no running the bases like today. Brains, not just guts. Brains and guts. That's it, or curtains. We don't make the play-offs, and next year, who knows? It'll all be about contracts and salaries, and they'll put us on a tight leash, I know that. . . . And why not? If we don't even know how to run the bases, what can they expect from a team that should've been the best in the league? I'm telling you the truth.

With his last words, the MANAGER *leaves the clubhouse and disappears. While he's been talking,* CHATO *has finished dressing in the clothes he's pulled out of a locker: blue jeans, lightweight shoes, T-shirt, jacket. Pensive and depressed, he moves to the area in which some pieces of furniture suggest the apartment where he lives. He opens the refrigerator, pulls out a can of beer, and sits at a table. Time goes by. The third base area lights up again. The third baseman is ready for the pitch, the play, looking expectantly toward home. The umpire, too. Again the sound of ball hitting bat, a sound of excitement from the crowd, but the area suddenly goes dark, as if erased by the presence of* CARMEN, *who enters the space where* CHATO *has been sitting at the table drinking his beer from the can.* CARMEN *is a young woman,* CHATO*'s wife. She's dressed and made up in preparation for going out.*

CARMEN. You're home? I didn't hear you. (CHATO *looks up, though barely, and otherwise doesn't move.* CARMEN *kisses him on the cheek, routinely.*) How did it go? Okay? (*She doesn't wait for an answer.*) I didn't think I'd see you, because they called me from that company, Sicón. Señor Martínez Reza, remember? It sounds like they've decided, like they're interested in the idea. Not just life insurance but cars, too. Amazing, don't you think? Because if I can sell the car policies and the life insurance too, it'll amount to . . . I've been working out the numbers. Something like twenty or thirty thousand, and to count on, I mean permanently. Just the annual renewals, that's what makes this so good, like Josefina told me, I'm so glad I listened to her, because she knew what she was talking about. . . . And Martínez Reza promised to recommend me to another company that's affiliated with theirs, an accounting firm, I think. Or else to their branch in Guadalajara which is expanding big-time. . . . If this works, we'll go out and celebrate, right? Like we planned. (*She looks at her watch, gets a bit of a shock.*) Wow, I'm late. (*She changes direction.*) Oh, where's my head? I forgot my purse. Where is it? What else am I forgetting? (CARMEN *disappears toward the interior of the apartment. Diffuse and ghostly light comes up in the area around third base. Once more the play, the throw to the third baseman, the sliding runner, the umpire signaling an out.* CARMEN *returns with a purse before the action is done.*) See you later, honey. (*She kisses him quickly.*) I'll be back, not too late. I don't think Martínez Reza will keep me long, but anyway I'll call if I'm going to be later than I think. Be good. I'll see you soon. (*She stops a few steps short of the exit, turns toward* CHATO.) Oh, listen. If Josefina calls, tell her I'm sorry; tell her I didn't call her because I had the urgent appointment at Sicón. Explain it to her. And I'll call her myself later. . . . And if my dad calls, I won't be long, and we're going to see him Sunday, like we planned, and he shouldn't worry. . . . Thanks, honey. I'll see you. And pray to God that this business works out. Cross your fingers. Bye."

CARMEN *exits, not to return.* CHATO *remains seated at the table, sunk into himself, finishing his beer. Then, after a long time, he crushes the can in his hand. He stands up and remains standing while he looks toward the ball field. Lights come up on the field, now brightly and sharply as in the first scene.* CHATO *watches while the third baseman waits expectantly for the play and listens to the murmur of the crowd. The third baseman and the umpire follow the flight of an imaginary ball. The third baseman runs to cover his bag. At that moment,* CHATO *tosses his crumpled beer can into the distance and runs at full speed toward the base. The throw comes in from the outfield. The third baseman catches the ball and leans down toward* CHATO *who is sliding in, still very fast. It's a close play. The umpire takes a few seconds to react. Still on the ground,* CHATO *looks up at the umpire. The umpire makes his decision and, with an emphatic gesture, signals the out.* CHATO *doesn't protest this time. He gets up and walks slowly, head hanging, toward the audience.*

Blackout.

ACKNOWLEDGMENTS

Many writers, readers, and translators pitched in to help with my search for stories and my efforts to contact their authors. I would like to thank Rafael Acevedo, Félix Julio Alfonso, Arturo Arango, Norberto Codina, Mylene Fernández, Daniel García, Javier González, Javier Lasarte, José Negroni, Achy Obejas, Barbara Paschke, Gabriel Saxton-Ruíz, and Katherine Silver as well as the acquisitions librarians of the University of California at Berkeley for their Latin American collection and the interlibrary loan staff at the San Francisco Public Library for their excellent service.

For their aid in pursuit of a publisher and early work on publicity I am grateful to Ellen Cassedy, Frances Dinkelspiel, Dan Fost, Tom Hallock, Andy Ross, and Joan Ryan. And, of course, to Robert Mandel and Irene Vilar for their belief in the book, as well as to Noel Parsons for careful copyediting.

It was, as always, both fun and extremely helpful to try out several of the translations on colleagues in the Bay Area Literary Translators Working Group as well as to read them at the annual Café Latino sessions at the conference of the American Literary Translators Association. All the authors graciously bore with my questions and suggestions.

Nancy Falk has been enthusiastic about this project from the beginning, as she has about so many of my other obsessions.

FURTHER READING

Complete novels, plays, or story collections by Vicente Leñero, Leonardo Padura, and Sergio Ramírez are available in English translation. Individual poems, stories, or plays by many of the other authors can be found in anthologies and periodicals. For baseball stories in particular, Ramírez's earlier tales "The Centerfielder" and "The Perfect Game" are in his *Stories* (Readers International, 1986, trans. Nick Caistor), and Arturo Arango's "Murder, According to My Mother-in-Law," is in Achy Obejas's collection *Havana Noir* (Akashic, 2011). Also in the crime fiction genre, the Cuban-Canadian novelist José Latour's *Havana World Series* (Grove, 2005) is a casino heist caper set against the background of Mafia-run gambling on the 1958 Yankees-Braves series.

For baseball fiction written in English by Latinos in the United States, see Robert Paul Moreira, *Arriba Baseball! A Collection of Latino/a Baseball Fiction* (VAO Publishing, 2013). In Spanish, the following anthologies are not easy to find but are well worth the trouble:

Jonrón 600: Primer concurso de cuentos sobre el béisbol (Secretaría de Estado de Cultura, República Dominicana, 2008), and

Círculo de espera: II concurso de cuentos sobre béisbol (Ediciones de Cultura, República Dominicana, 2012).

Leñero, Vicente, and Gerardo de la Torre. *Pisa y corre: Beisbol por escrito* (Alfaguara, Mexico, 2005). Stories, poems, plays, and memoirs.

Pacanins, Federico, ed. *El libro del beisbol: Cien años de pelota en la literatura venezolana* (El Nacional, 1998). Primarily essays, journalism, and poetry.

Terry Valdespino, Miguel, and Francisco García González, eds. *Escribas en el estadio: Cuentos cubanos de béisbol* (Editorial Unicornio, 2007, 2012).

On the history of Latin American baseball, in addition to the sources cited in the Introduction, some useful books in English are:

Bjarkman, Peter. *Baseball with a Latin Beat* (McFarland, 1994).

Gonzalez Echevarria, Roberto. *The Pride of Havana: A History of Cuban Baseball* (Oxford, 2001).

Jamail, Milton H. *Venezuelan Bust, Baseball Boom: Andres Reiner and Scouting on the New Frontier* (Bison Books, 2008).

Krich, John. *El Beisbol: Travel Through the Pan American Pastime* (Prentice Hall, 1989).

Kurlansky, Mark. *The Eastern Stars: How Baseball Changed the Dominican Town of San Pedro de Macorís* (Riverhead, 2010).

Ruck, Robert. *The Tropic of Baseball: Baseball in the Dominican Republic* (Bison Books, 1999).

Virtue, John. *South of the Color Barrier: How Jorge Pasquel and the Mexican League Pushed Baseball toward Racial Integration* (McFarland, 2008).

ABOUT THE EDITOR

Dick Cluster is a writer and translator in Oakland, California. He is the author of the novels *Return to Sender*, *Repulse Monkey,* and *Obligations of the Bone,* and of historical nonfiction including *History of Havana* (with Rafael Hernández) and *They Should Have Served That Cup of Coffee.* Recent fiction translations include Mylene Fernández Pintado, *A Corner of the World* (City Lights, 2014); Pedro de Jesús, *Frigid Tales* (Diálogos, 2014); and Aida Bahr, *Ophelias* (Cubanabooks, 2012). He has also translated scholarly and popular nonfiction from Latin America and Spain, and was Associate Director of the University Honors Program at the University of Massachusetts at Boston. He's a lifelong baseball fan, having transferred his loyalties over time from the Orioles to the Red Sox and now the Athletics—and always the Giants in the National League.